DEAR VALENTINE

OPPOSITES ATTRACT BOOK TWO

ROMEO ALEXANDER

CHAPTER ONE

"*U*n! Deux! Trois! Quatre!" Madame Roussou, the ballet instructor calls to the company. "Plie! Releve! Saute! Croise!"

I feel my legs work through the motions, as the rest of the company joins me in the cadence of her voice. Madame Roussou works her way down the line of dancers, pausing to correct the position of the feet, the arch of the back, or the sweep of the arms. She has a critique for every dancer, and when she pauses at me, I glance out of my peripheral, as she looks me up and down and commands, "Arch your back Colin. You need to lift from your core. You are shorter than a usual Danseur, but you need to present the image that you are just as tall!"

I work my core muscles, giving me an added half-inch of height as I plie again. It is well known through the company that the Adago will be continuous until Madame, as we call her, instructs us to stop. We let the movements flow from us in sweeping motions, as she continues down the line of dancers. I glance in the mirror to the left and straighten my shoulders and arch my back, giving the illusion of height. I couldn't stand out more in the floor to ceiling mirrors that line the entire studio. My auburn hair contrasts with the dark waves or platinum blondes of the other company members. My lesser height is also a source of contention, not only for the many dance instructors I've had growing up, but also with other dancers I've worked with.

I continue the movements as Madame moves her way back up the line. Her eagle eyes are sharp and, in this round, she is not as forgiving as the last. If any of her dancers have slipped into their bad form habits, she gives them a sharp rap on the offending appendage with her hard cane.

As she passes by me the second time, I make sure that I lift from my center, imagining that my navel is the apex of strings that are attached to my limbs and the ceiling is where the marionette sits, lifting me to my fullest height. Her gray eyes pause for a moment, but I am spared the sharp sting of wrath from her corrections. The beads on Madame's shawl jingle as she continues, and it is a sound that I have grown accustomed to over the last year. Somehow it is as natural as the cadence of the classical music that crackles from the record player. Madame is a stickler for tradition, having once trained in the finest Academies in France.

After her retirement from the Ballet de l'Opéra national de Paris, The Paris Opera Ballet, she was given a tenure here at Julliard in New York. She impressed upon the alumni the importance of classical training. She remained a permanent fixture, teaching at the school for the last several decades.

As the morning class passes, I feel my legs really start to burn. Madame instructs us to dig down deep, find our passion, and finish out the session strong as she has an important announcement. I continue lifting with a ballerina,

Katarina, who I had paired with before. I can feel my arm and leg muscles fatigue as she launches into another lift, and I execute the move flawlessly for the last time.

As I set Katarina down, she squeezes my arm in appreciation for a well-done class. I can see her cringing as she limps away worrying she might not be doing proper foot care in her pointe shoes. I sit against the back wall with the other danseurs, waiting for Madame to limp over. I rub at my sore calves and watch Katarina unlace her shoes and pull them off. The sheepskin padding she has put in to protect her feet is stained with blood and she winces as she peels off the layers. Open sores are visible on her feet from the pressure of the shoes.

"Katarina, how much have you been dancing this summer?" I ask quietly. Although there is a summer holiday, Madame has always encouraged us to continue dancing in between semesters so our feet don't end up just like this.

"Oh, you know me. I thought I could handle taking a few weeks off. Now I'm paying for it." She cringes as she applies antibiotics and then an ice pack to both feet. I nod, but make a mental note to speak with her further about proper foot care here at Julliard. Madame comes limping over, leaning heavily on her cane.

"Now, as most of you know, the Valentine's Day Virtuoso is the winter event here at our school."

Murmuring rumbles through the dancers, but quickly falls silent when Madame slams her cane on the wooden studio floor.

"There will be silence when I am speaking!" she shouts. "Ah, where was I? Oh, yes. The Valentine's Day Virtuoso. Every year, Julliard hosts many talented organizations here at this prestigious school. And every year, the drama programs are the ones to take center stage." She mutters something under her breath about the drama director, Mr. Schlewp. "The alumni have always been the attendees with their spouses at this event, and they have also been the ones deciding which acts are to be the highlighted event."

I feel like she is going somewhere with her speech, because she twirls her scarf's beads in her withered hands like she does whenever she is agitated. Much like the rest of the dancers, I'm beginning to wonder if she is about to announce that the drama program has taken over the show again as they have done in prior years. But what she says next has me and the rest of the company giving her our rapt attention.

"This year, some of the younger alumni came up with the brilliant idea to combine both the drama club and the ballet company."

There was absolute silence, until Angela, a prima ballerina spoke up. "Madame, they want us to do drama?" She twirls her black hair tightly into a coil and secures it at the back of her head in a severe bun.

"Yes and no, Angela. From what they tell me, the idea is to perform a musical with choreographed dancing that they wish to see coordinated with the drama students. Each organization will then perform their own respective acts, so we will of course perform one of the classics. The idea is to bring in more patrons to the event, as it raises money for the school. The venue will be large enough so that the alumni can have their night of romance, entertainment, and dining by candlelight while they watch the performances."

"What will the performance be, Madame?" Eric Reynolds, the class Primo asks. Madame turns to him, her wrinkled face twisting her harlot-red lipstick up into a smile. Eric has been her favorite as he is an exceptional dancer, tall and lithe, with hair equally as black as Angela's.

"I believe Mr. Schlewp has chosen a piece called *Rent*."

A collective wave of excitement washes through the crowd. Madame is known for her classical training and preference to choose pieces accordingly—*Romeo and Juliet* and *Swan Lake* being her two favorites. It will be interesting to know how she will adjust to a modern romantic piece with the added input of the drama director. It's also questionable if she understands that the piece caters to the LGBT audience, as the performance is based on the romance of a gay couple. I look at Katarina, wondering if she is as enthusiastic about this as I am.

The diversity of the piece could give me a shot at landing a primo role. Madame has always told me if it wasn't for my pesky Irish roots, cursing me with unnatural red hair that glows under the spotlights, and if I had been an inch taller, I would be flawless as a Primo. My genetics is something I've had to battle with all through my dancing career. But I've trained for hours and hours, making sure the moves I execute are flawless. With this piece, the stereotypical danseur is not necessarily the best fit. The main characters in *Rent* are an eclectic and diversified group of people.

I perk up immediately, listening for all the details. I've already decided to audition for the role of Tom Collins, the professor. I wonder how difficult it will be auditioning next to drama students. Will they be just as intimidated by the dancing roles as we are by the acting ones? There is some crossover between the two groups, but this piece could make a dancer's career shine.

"There will be a conjoined meeting of the two groups of students tomorrow to discuss tryouts and auditions. And then once the roles are cast, morning classes will be joint and afternoon classes will be to work on the piece in each area's respective classrooms. Your evening classes will be the normal routine," Madame finishes.

The class is dismissed for the lunch break. I walk with Katarina to the dining hall for lunch, my stomach growling. As we enter the dining room, I can see the uptick in excitement from the drama students as they buzz around one another, talking excitedly. They are an eclectic group of students. They stand out from the rest of the crowd. The musicians are always noticeable for having instruments with them while the dancers are almost always seen wearing tights, unitards, leotards, and leg warmers to keep their legs warm for the next round of dancing. However, a lot of the drama students, dress very differently. There are the bohemians, the gypsies, and the kids in jeans and t-shirts with a touch of something different.

One of the things I noticed first about the drama group is Gregor McCallum sitting in the middle of it. I duck my head and steal glances in his direction as Katarina and I chat and load up our trays. Gregor has always gone for a simple look of jeans and a t-shirt. He wears a tan fedora hat which he sometimes twirls in his hands and sometimes pulls low over his eyes making it hard to tell if he's watching you or not. He always seems to be the center of attention. Maybe it has something to do with the smile he perpetually has on his face. Or the fact that he's always laughing, whether it's joking with his friends or something he finds funny about life. It echoes through the dining hall, a large rectangular room with high windows and plain gray and white tables and chairs. Gregor's laugh cheers up the room whenever it booms out. Maybe that's why I find my attention drawn to the drama students: Gregor's presence.

I shake my head and bring my thoughts back to the present.

"I think you should try out for Mimi!" I tell Katarina.

"Yeah, why is that?" she asks. "Angela is going to get the part, anyway," she says bitterly.

I look sideways at Katarina who is loading her plate with sweets, carbs, and sugars. I look at my own and load it with proteins and greens.

"Katarina, what's wrong?" I watch the top of her dark head. She turns her face up to me and I consider her almond-shaped, brown eyes. They appear exotic to me, but maybe only because she is foreign.

"Nothing. Why?"

"Come on, pet. We're best friends. You can tell me anything. It just seems like you've been down since we got back to school…like, your heart isn't in this anymore."

She glances around nervously and then glares at me, "don't say that out loud! You want Madame all over my ass in classes?"

"Katarina, we all know she goes to her suite and takes a nap on lunch. She possibly even has a few nips from her bottle of port she carries in her tote bag that she thinks no one knows about. She's old. She can't hear anyway."

"For an old lady she still has senses like a hawk, or possibly two people who shall remain unnamed reporting back to her."

"Well I think if they report anything to her, it's going to be the atrocity of foods on that plate," I remark.

Katarina looks at her tray and shrugs. "I guess. It's just…I don't know. I've realized that dancing isn't going to last forever, you know?"

I ponder this over as we continue down the line and she slaps a healthy dollop of macaroni and cheese on her tray, followed by one of those sticky buns with the gooey glaze. She is going to have such a sugar crash later this afternoon and feel completely awful. She isn't wrong though. A dancer's career typically doesn't last long after they leave the school of performing arts. Ten years, maybe fifteen. It looks as though Katarina has already decided she would prefer to do something else with her life. The trouble is, her over zealous Russian parents are paying top dollar for her to attend this school.

I had to earn my way into the school by my Saint Patrick's Day performance of Lord of the Dance. I had grown up in Boston in an Irish family from Southie, and I had auditioned for the role in Michael Flatley's piece. At the time, in high school, I still hadn't narrowed my focus to one style of dance or the other, and I had miraculously landed the role. My father had been away at the docks working as a long-shoreman and my Mum had recognized that I am different, and had encouraged me to pursue my passion, dancing. Coming from a Catholic family, my other differences were never spoken about, but she had always known. As my mother, the love she had for me had her make peace with the fact that I am gay. She has never said a negative thing to me about it. When my brothers were old enough to work with Dad down at the docks, she insisted she needed a man at home to help her. So in secrecy, she had sent me to dance lessons. My sisters were my practice partners and never said a word to the rest of the family. They just encouraged me to continue practicing.

A recruiter for Julliard had attended the performance on opening night. He had been Madame Roussou's escort, and the two had approached me after. It had been a grueling session of answering questions about my dancing career and Madame had circled me many times, clicking her tongue at my less than ideal height and red hair. But the recruiter, Mr. Ward, had been enamored and convinced Madame that I was just the refreshing difference the school needed to bring into the fold. Last year had been brutal as Madame had refined my ballet skills. My feet had bled, my back had ached, and it seemed at every turn, I was shown up by Eric who had been the best of the best. Eric had been dancing since he was three and he had out-shown me in the sheer fact that he had the ideal body type. It had irked me all year. I had been practicing all summer to make up for it though and now I was determined to make the audition a real competition for him. I can empathize with how Katarina feels about Angela though.

"It won't hurt for you to try," I whisper. "If you decide that dance just isn't for you, maybe you could talk to your parents. I could be there with you if you like."

"Aww, that's so sweet of you Colin. But are you completely insane?" she asks staring at me horror struck.

I blink at her, wondering what part of what I just said was offensive.

"I've already had this conversation with my parents. They are adamant that I remain in dance. Anything other than the best is not acceptable to them," she states.

"Katarina, it is your life," I insist. "How are you going to be the best if this isn't what you want."

"I don't know. I guess I don't know what I want. I've always dreamed of being…"

"Being what?" I ask as we make our way to the back corner. Even in the performing arts schools, there seems to be cliques. Katarina and I aren't really with the in crowd of dancers, but we aren't outcasts either. The table we sit at gives us a perfect view of the dining hall. There are only a few chairs at this table which seems to be the oldest in the hall. There are scratches on the gray surface, and the best chairs had been stolen for other tables which were already overcrowded. I pick the wobbliest one, leaving the other gray chair for Katarina so that she won't topple over, if the legs finally do give out.

"Being an actress," she whispers like it's blasphemous.

I place my hand over my heart. "Ah! What say you? How has thee forsaken me!?" I cry as I stand and pirouette, dipping down onto one knee and holding my hands up to her in a manner of pleading.

Katarina laughs and shoves me, so I topple over. I stand and return to my seat, the whole performance barely registering on the populace's radar.

"Cut it out, Colin," she giggles. "You're being dramatic."

"Well, yeah. That's kind of the point of this place."

Katarina rolls her eyes and digs into her macaroni and cheese.

"Well, you know me," I say as I take a bite of my hard-boiled egg. "I'm on board with whatever you decide. But you better decide quickly because I'm pretty sure actresses need to be as thin as Prima Ballerinas. Have you seen those stick figures in Hollywood? Also, any more sticky buns and you're going to be like one of those dancing hippos from that Disney movie, Fantasia."

"Two things. One, are you fat shaming me?" she looks serious.

"Absolutely," I tease. She knows I am only joking and she knows I don't judge based on body size. But we are both realists in the world of dancing that it comes with the necessity of a certain body type.

"Yeah, you better be." She nudges my shoulder as I laugh.

"And the second?" I ask through a mouthful of spinach.

"There are dancing hippos in Fantasia?"

I glare at her and push my tray away.

"What?" she asks as I sit back and faux pout.

"I can't believe you have never seen Fantasia. That movie was the reason I decided I wanted to dance. Well, that and my inner desire to be cast in the Nutcracker so I can chase Angela around on stage as the evil Mouse King. Have you ever seen her shudder whenever someone mentions the mice extras? It's amazing."

"You have a black soul, Colin." Katarina is laughing so hard she's wiping tears from her eyes.

"You and me. Saturday night in my dorm. I'm sure Eric will be out with his fan club. We'll have a movie night and you can watch it with me."

"Alright. I'll give dancing hippos a chance. As long as there is popcorn."

"You are determined to see me have a heart attack. I just know it."

"Oh please, we need you to get some meat on those scrawny bones. How are you ever going to get a date with an ass that is streamlined with the rest of your body?" she taunts back.

"You slay me." I pull my tray back towards me and finish lunch. I don't comment on her food or potential for crisis this afternoon. It's her life and I just want to see my best friend happy.

I watch the crowds come and go, and my gaze wanders back to the drama group. Gregor is still the center of attention for that crew, and I have been feeling him since last year. I have seen him a few times in the halls and around the dorms, but never had the courage to talk to him. He's eating with his friends and laughing. His mocha skin is flawless and he tosses his dark head back and barks out a laugh at something one of his friends says.

"You should say hi to him. He's a pretty cool guy," Katarina remarks. I look around at her and frown.

"I don't have time to get involved with someone. I have to focus."

"Yeah, and then when you're old and gray and I'm the only one who visits you in the nursing home, remember that I encouraged you to live a little. Come on Colin, you've been crushing on him for over a year. Just go say hi, what is it going to hurt?"

"Well aren't you the pot calling the kettle black," I retort avoiding her question.

"Please, you so aren't the cliché."

I chuckle and stand up. "I'll catch you later. I'm going to hit the barre for some stretching before this afternoon."

"All work and no play…" Katarina smiles up at me. I tug her ponytail as I walk around the table and drop my tray off.

As I leave the dining hall, I catch a glimpse of Gregor and I pause a moment, getting caught in a trance just watching him tease one of his friends by grabbing their Gatorade and playing keep away. It's one of the things I have enjoyed most about observing Gregor, the way that he fools around with his friends. It's like there isn't a single care in the world when he is laughing and carrying on. I envy that carefree spirit. Sometimes when I fantasize about him, I imagine it's me he is smiling at and teasing. Katarina isn't wrong; I'd first noticed Gregor last year and had developed a silent and unseen crush. I'd imagined what it would be like to spend hours talking with him and just hanging out, laughing. The crush had developed into a small obsession so that whenever he walked into the dining hall, or I caught a glimpse of him at school, it was like a magnet is attached to my eyes and they immediately glance in his direction. The problem is, I can't afford to have distractions right now, and Gregor is one big, sexy distraction.

I sigh and push through the exit doors and make my way back to the studio to work on elongating my limbs with some barre exercises. I feel a small twinge of longing, but quickly shake it from my mind. I am determined and need to recenter my focus so that I can land this role at auditions.

CHAPTER TWO

he next day it feels foreign to me when I wake up and don't immediately put on my unitard and tights. I had grown accustomed to the attire in the year that I had been at school. I throw on a t-shirt and some sweatpants and head down to the auditorium to congregate with the other dancers. I walk in and sit in one of the back rows and wait for Katarina. I find it amusing that the dancers and the drama students are all sitting on opposite sides of the auditorium with their respective friends. For a group of students who are going to share talents and work with one another, the segregation is an obvious sign for future issues.

Katarina slumps down in her seat beside me as Madame sits primly in a chair next to the podium. A wiry, balding, Mr. Schlewp shuffles through some notes at the podium.

"How are you feeling?" I murmur. Yesterday had been brutal on her. Sure enough, the sugar crash had left her feeling ill and with little energy. With the continued lifts that we had been practicing, and the arabesques and the grande jetés, the class had her collapsing onto the sofa in my dorm as we worked on the academic schoolwork.

"I feel like I put a dumpster in my stomach," she whispers.

"So, no need to mention all the garbage you ate?"

"You just did."

Katarina groans as the microphone is turned on. The whole auditorium cringes as the loud squeal emits from the sound booth. As it is turned on, Mr. Schlewp clears his throat.

"Greetings. I am excited to deliver the details regarding the Valentine's Day Virtuoso this year. Madame Roussou and I are pleased to work together to bring an exciting new form of entertainment for our alumni." He turns and indicates to Madame sitting beside the podium. The look she has on her face is anything but pleased. Her lips are pinched as if she has tasted something sour and that does not bode well for her temper. Madame looks around briefly, flashing a grimace that mimics a smile.

I catch some of the drama students whispering to each other and laughing, and it bothers me. They think they have her all figured out, but they have no idea the dedication she has to the school and the dancers. I pretend, as I notice Gregor whispering with one of his friends, that he isn't like the others. Sometimes living in my own head and fantasizing about a man can be maddening. My attention is drawn back to the stage when Katarina nudges me.

"This year, in addition to the drama students performing a small play and the ballet company performing...eh...a piece that Madame Roussou will decide on at a later time, we have decided to do a joint musical, Rent. I'm sure some of you have heard of or seen the musical. It is a modern romance featuring alternative lifestyles and we think it will add an eclectic piece to the evenings dossier."

Madame snorts at his attempted pronunciation of a French word, and it's the dance student's turn to snicker. I get the feeling that this performance is going to see a few disputes of differences before it is through, but I'm still excited.

"Auditions will be held to cast the roles. Anyone is eligible for any of the roles. It doesn't matter if you are a dancer or actor, we will decide upon a mix of students from both groups and then a string of alternates to back study in case anything happens. This is normal and I'm sure you will all agree, each and every one of us will contribute to helping our fellow students perform to the best of their abilities. We expect the drama group to assist the dancers with their acting abilities, and likewise we would appreciate the input from the dancers for the choreographed pieces within the musical."

Mr. Schlewp falls silent and looks around. No one says anything, so he turns to Madame.

"Is there anything you would like to add?"

I feel almost sorry for him because a gleam enters her eye as she stands up and takes over the microphone.

"As my students are aware, I run a strict class schedule. Practice in the morning, afternoon, and an evening session. I expect, as we need to maintain the integrity of this school's reputation, that any student who is cast into a role will willingly sacrifice their time and devote it to making this musical shine. That includes weekends as well. My evening classes will be left for the preparation of the classical piece. I have chosen Swan Lake, which has been performed at every Valentine's Day Virtuoso, and flawlessly I might add."

There is a collective groan from the audience. It is no wonder the alumni decided on a new chain of events for the evening. I see Eric and Angela turn to each other, already whispering about their roles. They had performed it last year and would no doubt do so again this year. Katarina nudges me with her knee and I turn my attention back to Madame who is glowering at the whispering drama students. They quickly quiet under her withering stare, realizing she is serious when she indicates she is a stickler for rigid schedules. Everyone knows she is set in her way of doing things and commands respect. It's going to be interesting watching the drama students bend to her will.

"Now, what was I saying? Oh, yes. From what I understand, Rent is an unusual performance, and well outside my usual decision of a classical piece. That doesn't mean I am not willing to give the same dedication to teaching the piece to its full effect. For auditions for the dance segment, I expect that you will prepare two pieces, one classical and the other a segment of your choice to demonstrate your capabilities and fluidity between dance styles. Auditions will be in one week, and then a week after that, the roles will be cast. I'm sure Mr. Schlewp has a reading for you of some kind as well."

Mr. Schlewp stands and leans in towards the microphone, causing Madame to lean away and look at him incredulously for invading her personal space.

"Eh, yes. After performing your dance numbers, I will have you read for the part you are auditioning for, and then as a second piece, as Madame Roussou has indicated, please prepare a statement as to why you wish to be cast in this piece."

He sits back down, and Madame clears her throat.

17

"I, of course, will be considering not just a first line of dancers, but a second string and possibly a third as well. There is a lot that can happen between now and February, and it's best to be prepared. I do believe in drama they are called understudies."

She says the word understudy like whoever is cast as such is the absolute last resort, the dregs of the barrel so to speak. I look at Eric again who is nodding absentmindedly, like he is agreeing with every word she says, not because he thinks he would ever be second string, but because he feels it is necessary to discriminate from the absolute best, and he has no cause for concern. It irritates me to see him looking so unconcerned, like he is entitled to every Danseur primo part just because he has been cast in them before. Now he isn't just competing against me and a few other male dancers, but he is competing against the drama club as well, and I'm hoping they can bring a challenge to the floor, just as much as I know I can.

"On a final note, evening classes will be dismissed this week for you to have time to prepare your dances. That is, my classes will be dismissed. I believe Mr. Schlewp already permits his students free reign during that time, to participate in leisurely activities."

Mr. Schlewp tugs at the tie on his collar and nods at Madame as the dancers snicker and the drama students make mocking gestures of laziness and feigned interest.

After she finishes her speech that some of us have heard thousands of times about perfection, integrity, dedication and hard work, Mr. Schlewp presses a button on the podium, bringing down the projector screen, and the auditorium crackles with the powering up of the speakers. The music blares through the room. Madame had tsk'd at having a screening of the movie, preferring to let the story shine through the performance, but Mr. Schlewp had insisted on it for the benefit of his drama students, and since they were going to show it to one group, it was only fair it be shown to all.

I sit back and cross my legs, letting my gaze fall to the back of Gregor's head. He's whispering with a friend and I am content to watch him for the rest of the screening, except when he looks back and catches me staring at him. I quickly duck my head and let my eyes wander all over the theater with as much of a mask of stupor as I can muster, but I feel his dark eyes boring into the side of my face as I let my gaze wander back to the screen.

After a few moments, I hear Katarina slump, her head on my arm as she lightly snores. The sound is drowned out by the volume from the movie's sound, and with the lights dim, no one notices her. I pat her knee and grab my fleece jacket from the opposite chair and drape it over her shoulders. I sneak a peek back at Gregor, but he is watching the screen and a spike of jealousy runs through me as his friend leans over and whispers something in his ear. I try to clear my mind of thoughts of him. It will only serve as a distraction for the upcoming week. I have so many ideas for the unique piece that I begin to mull over. I need to do something that will really stand out. I'm not concerned with the ballet piece. I have choreographed and performed hundreds of them to perfection by now. I am thinking I should go back to my basics, what I started out being good at.

Although a tap dance won't be ideal for this piece, I think I should consider what piece got me accepted to Julliard. The Lord of the Dance is essentially a battle between the Lord of Light and the Prince of Darkness. The musical Rent is the battle and struggle of members of the LGBT community and the AIDS epidemic. I own a pair of street shoes, or rather, jazz shoes, as they are called. Their flexibility will enable me to move freely, as the vision I begin to form in my head becomes a choreographed piece of demonstrating an internal battle and interacting with outside forces. There are plenty of props available to work with on the stage. Only a few will be necessary to interact with for this. I can incorporate the heart-wrenching sweeping moves of classical ballet to demonstrate the internal struggle, and use the freeform dance to interact with my surroundings.

I'm almost anxious for the film to be done so I can get to work on perfecting the piece, but it is nice to have a break from the constant grueling sessions from Madame.

Katarina grunts in her sleep, and wipes drool on the back of her hand and lets it fall back into her lap. I'll have to tease her later for being gross, but I give the top of her head a quick kiss and finish watching the movie with the rest of the classes.

Once the movie is done, we are dismissed to lunch and I shake Katarina awake. She glares at me as she fixes her pony-tail which had gone lopsided on her head.

"Feeling better?" I ask as she rubs her eyes.

"Yeah. What did I miss?" she asks.

"The whole film," I explain as she hands me back the fleece.

"Alright then, hopefully you took notes, and I can look at yours later!" She grins at me. She smacks her lips together and frowns.

"What's the matter?"

"I'm super thirsty. Let's go get lunch so I can get a water."

"Doesn't surprise me," I tease. "You drooled buckets onto your t-shirt."

I point to the wet spot on her shirt and she crinkles her nose at it.

"Gross."

"I know you are, but I still love you. Come on luv." I stand and sling my dance bag over my shoulder.

Katarina collects her things and we head to the doors at the back of the auditorium. As we step out into the glaring over-head fluorescent lighting, I hear a sneering voice behind us.

"She's even worse looking under these lights than when she is open mouthed and drooling on your arm."

I turn and see Angela and Eric exiting the auditorium.

"Angela, always a pleasure," I murmur. Her cat-like eyes glare at me as she looks me up and down, and then does the same raking once over of Katarina.

"Well, someone's been divulging in too much pleasure. Any more sweets Katarina, and I don't know how Colin is going to be able to lift you off the floor."

Katarina glowers at her, but says nothing. I quickly change the subject, before it gets too catty.

"What part are you trying out for Angela?" I ask.

"Well obviously one of the leads. Mimi of course. She's the female lead. But, I can also identify with Joanne, I suppose."

"Why, because you have rich and powerful parents?"

"And that character is Ivy league and a lawyer."

"Yep, and nothing screams shark like you do Angela."

I loop Katarina under the arm and turn back around to leave.

"Who are you auditioning for?" Eric sneers. I don't bother to turn around and answer him. Whatever snide thing he has to say will only infuriate me more.

I hear it again, "Who are you auditioning for?" I turn on my heel, ready to snap at him, and see Gregor standing there. Eric and Angela push past us and keep walking, laughing at us from over their shoulder.

"I'm going to just…" Katarina trails off.

"Ah…" I start. "Sorry, I'm auditioning for the lead. Mark, is the character's name. I'll second for the professor character, Tom Collins."

"That's cool. Any idea what you are going to do for your second dance?" Gregor asks. His eyes are so brown they look like pools of chocolate. His skin is mocha, and shines under the light, making him look positively edible to me. I get lost in staring at him, and when he gets that weirded out look on his face, I snap out of it.

"Oh, yeah. Sorry. I think a mixed dance. A little classy, a little freestyle."

"Sound like a solid plan. Well, I'll see you around," he murmurs and turns in the other direction, heading for his group of friends who are waiting for him. I notice the guy that had been whispering in his ear glare at me from over his shoulder. I turn and walk away toward the dining hall, completely perplexed as to what that was all about. In all this past year, Gregor had never once shown an interest in me. Nevermind a desire to chat me up in the hall before. I had seen him around last year, but figured he was running with his crowd and wouldn't give me the time of day. Not that I was, or am, looking for anyone right now. I have to give my focus completely over to the dance if I ever want a shot at the lead role.

When I enter the dining hall, I find Katarina in our usual corner. The black and gray plastic seats are scattered around, as we are the only two who sit in this corner of the dining hall. I get in line and load up my tray as I look around to wait for Gregor and his friends to come into the dining hall, but they don't show up.

"What was that all about?" Katarina asks.

"What do you mean?" I startle and look over at her.

"Just that, in all this time, Gregor has never talked to you before. Did he ask you out?" She nudges my shoulder as I shove her playfully back.

"No. He just wanted to know what part I am trying out for."

"That's it? That's all he wanted to know?" Her tone is dry.

"Yeah, why?" I ask through a mouthful of kale.

"Because, he can easily figure that out at tryouts, silly." She sighs in exasperation.

"So?"

"So, you think he took the time out of his schedule to come talk to you about what everyone around here talks about? School and performances? He never once spoke to you before and now all of a sudden, it's so important for him to know your thoughts. You really are dense sometimes Colin."

"I...I...well why didn't he say he was interested in talking about something else then?" I demand. She rolls her eyes at me.

"You're a guy. You know how you all roll. Very rarely do you actually say you're interested in something. Sometimes you point and grunt, other times you purposefully ignore the very thing you are interested in. Don't ask me to understand the macho man thing, because I don't. But yeah. He was trying to tell you he was interested."

"Well, I don't get it either. But there you have it. I blew it. So, can we move on? I want to try out a couple of moves before class this afternoon."

"You go ahead. I'm going to continue enjoying this nice, cheesy piece of pizza."

"Yeah you do that. I'll leave you to the love of your life then." I give her cheek a peck and she punches my shoulder, but looks happily back at her pizza. I roll my eyes in turn and head to the studio.

24

CHAPTER THREE

hat afternoon, the session goes by at a snail's pace. Madame has us begin with the basics for Swan Lake, which everyone knows but she puts us through the paces anyway. When it is time for the run-throughs, it is evident who she has decided are the leads, because she places Angela and Eric in the front of the class to take position.

I watch as the two of them move around one another with a fluidity that can only be described as singular. Even though they are two separate bodies, they move as one. It is apparent why Madame prefers them to any other, because there is something more to the way they dance with each other, an understanding of some kind that links them in a way that just performing the moves doesn't. If it weren't for the fact that everyone knows Eric is openly gay, I would guess that the understanding or emotion in the way they dance together is passion, but it is something altogether and entirely different.

When the class is over, it feels strange to me to have an entire evening of free time. I meet with Katarina in the dining hall for dinner and she eats quickly, taking off without explaining where she is going. Like most people, she is probably going to prepare a dance and wants to be alone to think it through.

When I get back to the studio, there are several students already working and I realize I am never going to be able to focus in there, so I go in search of another empty studio.

As I walk through the hallways, I hear a number of different songs playing from the rooms and occasionally glance at snippets from the choreography they are putting together. I hear and see a lot of different styles and suddenly I am wondering if mine will be good enough.

I can't find an empty classroom, so I try the auditorium one last time before deciding on my back up plan. When I enter the large room, I'm relieved to see no one in there. I hurry down to the stage and hop up. It feels massive to me with no one else present, and no other dancers performing with me. The wooden floor is scuffed and marked from hundreds of performances being done.

I circle the stage a few times, trying to get a feel for the atmosphere. I haven't chosen a song yet, but I drop my bag and quickly pull on my jazz shoes. I pirouette a few times across the stage, allowing my body to loosen up and for inspiration to come over me. I notice a folding chair stage left behind the curtain, where someone in charge of dropping the curtains had been sitting. I pick it up and set it in the middle of the stage, allowing the vision of a bench in the city to cloud my mind. I fuse the fantasy with the reality of the chair being there. I imagine that like so many benches around New York, this is the one I will be interacting with and this is the one that will be an obstacle for me.

I dance around the chair, spinning faster and faster and then pull out so that I grab the chair by its back and sit down, exhausted. I've seen this pose by so many strangers throughout the city. The benches in the park, the bus stop benches, the benches on the streets. So many people have sat on them, unaware of the lives that have come and gone from that one spot. I let my weight fall away as my feet pick me up from my perch. I let the dance communicate that I am leaving my trials and worries behind. The freestyle, I let my body move into turns, into something that is about freeing myself. The anger towards my family for not allowing me to be open about who I am. The anger at how grueling and hard it is to shine brightly as the best dancer, but only to be shown up by Eric again and again. And finally, all of the emotions that come with openly admitting that I am gay, all come pouring out of my body as I dance.

I reach the edge of the stage and stop, holding my arms up and backing away on pointed, arched feet. I shuffle backwards as if I had just cast it all from the stage and there is a new feeling that enters me as I sashay backwards. Elation, happiness and wonder begin to enter my dance. I picture Katarina's face in my mind, and I perform a Batterie. I feel warm and welcome as I think of our candor and honesty with one another. I feel love for having a best friend who brings humor and fun to my life.

Then I think of Gregor. I don't know why, but his face enters my mind. I perform a Déboulé. As I hurtle my way up the stage, I wonder if I am trying to flee from the image of him in my mind, or if I am performing the move because with the thought of him, my heart races and I feel my spirit lift and take flight. I stop at the edge of the stage again. I shake my head, trying to clear it of thoughts of Gregor. He can't be a factor in this dance. It needs to be about interacting with the environment and battling the will. I snort at the irony of that thought, because it is a battle of my will to get him from my mind. I bend, taking in a few deep breaths and wipe the sweat from my brow. I circle the stage one more time, but freeze when I come back around, and the very person I was trying not to think about, is leaning on his forearms at the base of the stage in the center. Gregor's eyes bore into mine as I stare at him. It takes me a few moments to think of something to say.

"Did you need the stage? I'm sorry, I couldn't find a quiet place to practice and think, but if you need the stage to practice…"

He doesn't say a word, but puts both hands flat on the stage and uses his muscles to hoist himself up. I look stage left and right, subconsciously seeking an escape. I have never been alone with him. What could he possibly want? As he walks closer to me, I am unaware at first that I am walking backward, trying to escape his advance. I force myself to hold still as he draws nearer.

"Sorry," I say again. "Did I do something wrong? I didn't think there were school rules about not using the stage. Is it drama practice tonight?" I realize I am babbling but he just smiles.

"Calm down." His voice is like rich, smooth, honey. I stop talking as he finally stops walking toward me, only inches from me. I inhale, without realizing. His aftershave is musky and rich. I sway on my feet. It must be the blood flowing so swiftly through my body from the exercise. I look around for my water bottle and spot it at the far end of the stage. It looks so far but it would definitely be seen as me running away if I walk toward it. I take a few deep breaths, calming myself down. "You've got some intense moves. I was watching the dance," he says in a low voice.

I stare up at him, not sure how to respond to the fact that he has been watching me. "Um, thanks?" I try.

He chuckles and continues. "Any idea what you're going to use for music?"

"I was thinking Beethoven's 5th Symphony," I supply. I had been wondering myself. I know it needs to be something intense, angry and fast paced.

"I've heard it," he says. "Can I offer some advice though?"

"Yeah sure, what's that?" I ask. It takes me by surprise that he knows the classical genre. I wonder where he has heard it.

"Don't choose music that you normally dance to," he offers. I crinkle my brow, curious and confused as to why he'd say that.

"What do you mean?" I wonder.

"It's just, I watch you dancer types sometimes. I could never be a dancer like that, but I love to dance, you know what I'm saying."

"You want to be a Danseur?" I can't keep the incredulity out of my voice.

"Not necessarily, but I do love to dance. The thing is, you always go for classical pieces. I know Madame Roussou is classically trained, but that's not what is going to make you stand out. I chose drama because there are so many different styles you can choose from when auditioning for plays and musicals. There's so many variations of music and pieces that can speak to a person, you know?"

I nod, as understanding begins to dawn on me. "I wasn't picked because of ballet," I explain. "I was the lead in The Lord of the Dance. Madame Roussou happened to be in attendance with a recruiter from the admissions department, and they approached me after. But the piece is performed with tap dancing."

He shakes his head. "Alright, alright. See, that's what you need to focus on: what made you stand out. I've been walking around the school, thinking about what I could do to have the same effect for myself, and all I see is dancers performing traditional pieces. Those aren't going to be the ones to get the roles. Eric and Angela, they'll be cast into leads automatically because they look the part of the ballet people. But if you want a real shot at getting the lead role in the musical, you have to stand out and not in your appearance. I imagine you get a lot of flack for that red hair," he grins at me.

"Yeah, I do," I agree.

"You need to make your dance stand out man."

"Thanks for the advice." I look up at him from under my lashes. I hadn't realized how tall he is until I am standing next to him. He's at least a few inches taller than I am, but his height and more pronounced muscle mass are sexy. My brain kicks into overdrive and I suddenly envision what it would be like to be held in his arms.

"No problem," he murmurs. I feel him rather than see him take a step closer to me as he says it. I had quickly glanced back at the floor after staring too long at him. I feel my pulse quicken and I rub my palms on my sweatpants. I work to control the urge to step back.

"Can I give you another piece of advice?" he asks. His voice is almost a whisper near my ear and I swallow hard as I try not to turn my head and steal a quick kiss. "Don't apologize all the time for being around. If I didn't want to be near you, I wouldn't have come to find you," he murmurs. I feel the brush of his lips against my ear and I shudder, unable to repress the electric jolt that even the softest contact had sent shooting through my body. I squeeze my eyes shut as I sway on my feet.

"I've been watching you for a while now," he confesses and my eyes pop open.

"You have?" I squeak and clear my throat.

"Yeah, and then I decided to come talk to you after I caught you staring at me this morning." He smiles as he admits this to me. Before I can pull away, his arm shoots up and he cups the back of my head as he draws me in for a kiss. Being encased in his arms is just as I had fantasized, and his kiss is even more intoxicating as he lowers his head to mine. His lips are large and soft, and I feel completely engulfed in him as his tongue slips out and touches my lips. I cling to his hoodie and tilt my head back, allowing him to dominate the situation and control the kiss. I try to arch my back to hold the erection that had thickened the length of me in my fitted sweatpants. There's no denying that it is there. I had gotten hard the second his lips touched my ear, and the kiss is driving my arousal into a frenzied state.

He senses my hesitation and uses his other arm to wrap around my waist, drawing me flush against him. I jump in surprise when I feel the thick length of him pressed against me through his own jeans. He groans as we come in contact and I quiver as he deepens the kiss. We stand there, pressed together and grinding against one another.

He only breaks the kiss off as his lips trail down over my jaw and neck and I moan as I feel his hot tongue run over my Adam's apple. The vibrations from his mouth send shivers of pleasure racing along under my skin. I feel the tension begin to throb between my thighs as his touches hit my nerves and shoot through my system, sending signals in a cascade of pleasure downward. I dance and jiggle in his arms when his palms cup me from behind through my sweats and begin to massage. The contact causes us to press harder into one another in the front and I can't escape the sensations which have started to spiral out of my control.

A dull ache has begun down below, and the feeling is causing the ache to spread through the length of me as it throbs and tingles. I break off the kiss, afraid I am about to embarrass myself for my lack of control.

"Gregor!" I surprise myself when it comes out high-pitched and a cry of need. He nips at my earlobe again, having found the spot that is extra sensitive and sets me to jumping in his arms. His teasing is maddening and just as I'm about to lose control and be lost in his arms, a voice calls from the podium area,

"Not interrupting anything, am I?" Eric's sneer sounds through the whole stage and I jump back. Gregor is more casual to let go as I struggle breaking free. I notice his eyes are dangerous as he stares at me. Raw lust is shimmering in his gaze, but as he turns to Eric, it changes to something threatening.

"What do you want, Eric?" he demands. I take the opportunity to dash across the stage and escape. I pick up my water bottle, my bag, jump down off the stage and run up the aisle to the door.

I jog all the way to my room and slam the door, locking myself in. I pace my room with my arms above my head, afraid to touch my hypersensitive skin as I try to breath some control back into my body. I look around, hating the plain beige walls and navy blue bed set. They offer no visual distraction for me to get caught up in and forget about what had just happened. I spend so little time in here, I hadn't taken the time to decorate or hang posters or anything. The room is small with a single bed and dresser. I have a small t.v. I never watch on top of it, and a bean bag chair in the corner that Katarina sits on, for the rare times we do have time to just hang out and relax.

The ache between my thighs is maddening and I usually don't spend much time thinking about sex or anything like that, because I prefer to focus on more important things like my dancing and college career. Sure, I have the occasional session on my own in the bathroom or in bed, but no one has ever made me feel this intensely before, and as I pace, I realize it kind of scares me. I don't want to lose focus on what's important. Gregor McCallum is a distraction I don't need right now.

When I am finally calmed down enough to sit, I do so grate-fully. I lie back on my bed and let my hand trail down the length of my stomach. I'm irritated with him now. Is this a ploy to get me distracted to be able to win the casting role? Anger surges through me as I realize it worked. I'm so hard there is no way that it's going away unless I do something about it. I turn and punch my pillow in frustration. Maybe that had been his plan all along, to distract me in order to get the stage all to himself. I mean, what do I really know about Gregor except, he's easy on the eyes and looking at him makes me fantasize about being in a relationship with him. What bugs me is every time I do catch glimpses of him, he's smiling, and he looks like he is happy. Like being here at school isn't hard work and he's just having fun. Maybe that's the attraction, a man who can just be causal, carefree, and have fun.

I think about the amount of times I have smiled in Madame Roussou's class and realize, it isn't often. The classes are hard and I'm usually so focused and determined to achieve perfection, it isn't fun, it's just hard work.

I cup myself as I fantasize about Gregor's smile and the feel of being trapped in his arms. It doesn't take me long to finish. I have never had a boyfriend, despite knowing I'm gay. I've kissed a few guys, but nothing ever led to anything because I use my dancing as a way to shut them out, so I don't have to get involved with anyone. Damn Gregor. He'd used the one thing I used as a shield as a way to get to me.

When I'm done, I go and shower, letting the hot water clear my mind and relax me so that when I enter my dorm again, I fall asleep almost immediately. I don't see the light on my phone indicating there is a message for me from Katarina, and it isn't until the next morning that I find out what she had been trying to get a hold of me for.

CHAPTER FOUR

"*W*hy is everyone staring at me?" I ask her as I sit down to breakfast.

"Well maybe if you had texted me back last night," she starts, "you would know that the entire school knows about the kiss between you and Gregor," she finishes.

I stare at her in horror as I gaze around the room and see all the students looking at me and whispering. I quickly duck my head and look at my plate of food, which suddenly looks unappetizing and like a mass of gelatinous goo that if I were to put in my mouth, would make me instantly sick to my stomach.

"What happened?" she pries, and I shake my head. I really don't want to think about it, and now I really don't want to talk about it. "Colin," she says gently. I swallow hard and try to focus on taking a spoonful of oatmeal and shoving it in my mouth. It's a difficult feat, as my hand is shaking so much.

Which one was it? I wonder to myself. It could have been

either Eric or Gregor. It is obvious why Eric would spread the news about the kiss around school. It's no secret we barely tolerate each other. But if it was Gregor? He could have told his drama friends and I don't know them very well. Any one of them could have started the rumor chain. If it was Gregor who told people, then maybe I was right after all, and he was using it as a way to distract me. I feel my face burn with embarrassment.

"He wouldn't do that to you," Katarina says quietly. I look up, startled by her words.

"What?" I croak. I'm trying so hard to suppress the tears I can feel burning in my eyes, it's making my throat hurt.

"I've hung out with Gregor a few times. I told you that. Last year, I went to a party with the drama kids and he was still dating that guy he was sitting next to yesterday, Seth, I think is his name. Anyway, they were there, and I watched him interact with him. He's really protective of the guy he's with," she says.

"If they are exes, why were they sitting next to each other yesterday?" I blurt out before I can stop myself. Even I can't keep the jealousy from my voice and she raises an eyebrow as I hang my head again, and force another spoonful of oatmeal into my mouth.

"Haven't you ever heard the expression, 'we can still be friends'? Wait, never mind, I forgot I was talking to Mr.-I-Don't-Date-Because-It-Takes-Away-From-My-Dancing-And-All-The-Time-I-Spend-Watching-Myself-In-The-Studio-Mirror."

"Ouch, damn Katarina, that was mean," I mumble into my oatmeal.

"Well, it's true. I guess Seth is having a hard time letting go and is still pushing Gregor to remain friends and all that, hoping he can convince him to get back together with him or something. Not that Gregor ever will, I guess there was a question about Seth and Eric hooking up and Gregor just doesn't go for that sort of thing. Too much drama for the drama guy. He likes his men faithful. But you would know that if you had a social life. Instead you spend all your time just practicing, practicing, practicing," she chides.

Her words are true, but it doesn't make them sting any less. I jump up from the table, unable to stomach the food any longer and I snap, "Well, excuse me if some of us take our career seriously. Just because you can't decide which side of the fence you're on, ours or theirs, don't give me crap about taking my decision seriously!"

I push wildly through the crowd, trying to escape so I can feel like I am alone with my thoughts. I stop when I see Eric's sneering face come into view. He's blocking the exit and I demand, "get out of the way, Eric."

"That was some kiss, O'Shea," he starts. I step to the right to go around him and he pairs the movement. "Where you going in such a hurry? You and Gregor meeting backstage for some more one-on-one time? I think we should just tell Madame and Mr. Schlewp there is no need to perform a romantic drama, the two of you would do just fine on your own," he taunts.

"What are you, in second grade?" I hear Katarina behind me. "Who cares if they kissed, Eric? Just get out of the way, you're holding up the exit."

I see it then. The answer to her question is all over Eric's face. He's jealous. I begin to say something nasty, about finally having something he doesn't. It makes sense, if he really was the cause of Seth and Gregor breaking up. He would have done it intentionally to get Seth out of the way to get to what he wanted, Gregor. I am spared having to say anything because a cold chill runs down my spine when I hear Gregor say, "get out of his way, Eric."

I absolutely refuse to turn around and look at him. Eric snarls, "see you in class," and then steps aside, and I bolt for the door. I feel Katarina behind me as I turn to go outside for some air, instead of back to the confines of my dorm room. There is still half an hour before class begins and I take great gulps of air as I rush down the sidewalk. The busy city surrounds us, and the cadence of sounds that hit my ears somehow soothes me as I let myself become lost in the din.

I snort with laughter, which causes Katarina to look at me with a worried expression.

"Are you ok?" she asks.

"Yeah, it's just, have you ever noticed that the one thing I have tried to do is stand out. Be noticed by people for my abilities and differences, but at the same time have them not notice my differences like red hair instead of dark or short stature instead of tall and lean? I mean, that my whole existence is proving that I'm different, but in the right way. The irony of it is, it was what I was trying to accomplish with my dance last night. Portraying that internal conflict, you know? And here's the second punch-line. The one place I go to calm down when I can't deal with it, is to get lost in and become just another face in the crowd. It makes me feel better to blend in and not stand out when it comes to the fact that I'm gay. Double irony, don't you think?"

Katarina nods her head and then says, "I get it, I think. I'm not gay, but I get that you've hid that from people like your family for so long, and then to suddenly have it all over school must be hard, even though people know already. There are so many students here who are. It isn't really something that is talked about a lot because it's well, normal. But to have it so blatantly pointed out was a bit harsh. So yeah, I think I get it. But look, it's over. Old news by tomorrow. You just need to put your dancing shoes back on and get back in there and do what you do best, Colin," she urges.

I stop walking and give her a hug. "Thanks, Katarina. I don't know what I would do without you."

"Dance yourself until you were dead probably. You need to be grounded in reality by someone. And I'm just the person to tell you dancing isn't everything. You have other stuff, Gregor stuff, to think about now."

I deadpan her with my stare. "He's the last thing I need to focus on. Don't think it hasn't occurred to me that he did it just to throw me off my game or get the stage to himself."

"I told you, he isn't like that. You should give him a chance," she insists. I shrug and turn back around, having walked several blocks down from the school just to get out of sight of it for a while.

"I don't know about investing time; it was just a kiss. But hey, I'm sorry I snapped at you earlier. It was a shitty thing to do and you're my best friend, I shouldn't have done that."

"It's all good. I just want you to think about one thing though."

"Yeah what's that?" I ask.

"If it was only a kiss, then why was it so influential to have you this worked up that you run away from school and snap at your best friend?"

I stop walking but she doesn't. I glare at her back a moment before I jog to catch up with her and head to class. I look out of the corner of my eye and see she is smiling, but I change the subject.

"What do you think it will be today? Lifts again?"

"Nah, I think we're long overdue for some calisthenics or a stretching session." Thankfully, she shows me mercy by not pressing her last insight. But the annoyance burns because she does have me wondering all day about her question.

Madame Roussou is all over me in class for being unfocused. Eric doesn't say anything further but has pointed, whispered conversations with Angela who laughs every time I walk by. The day drags on and by the time we are dismissed from the afternoon session, my calves are burning from the constant tapping of Madame's cane on the back of them to snap me back to attention.

I decide to skip dinner and the evening session of finding an empty studio and I purposefully steer clear of the auditorium. My earlier conversation has me at the train station, purchasing a ticket to head up to Boston, to visit my family. There are sometimes when it is just a good idea to head home for a spell and see family, and I know my Mum will be putting on dinner about the time I arrive. I don't call or text to say I'm coming. She never turns me away when I show up, the question is whether once I get there, I will hesitate at the door, wondering if it's worth the withering stares of some of my brothers to show up at home. The worse one is the passive face of my Dad, who has never said a negative word about my decision to accept the scholarship to dance, or my sexuality, but he has never said an encouraging or positive word either. I realize I am making the trip home to again gauge his reaction to all of it, needing to know whether he approves of me or not, and I don't text because I don't know if I'll have the courage to knock on the door and find out.

CHAPTER FIVE

*W*hen I get home, I take the subway to the south side of Boston. I pull a hoodie out of my backpack and pull it on, concealing my face. I had changed into jeans and sneakers before leaving. The three-hour train ride had taken what seemed like forever, but I arrived home around five-thirty.

It makes for walking up to the front door easy, because I know Dad, Liam, Seamus, and Patrick are all still down at the docks, leaving Mum, Kathy, Sarah, and Collene at home. I jog up the steps of the old Brownstone building and let myself in through the front door. Dad and Mum had worked hard to purchase the entire downstairs of the apartment building, in order to have room for our large family. They paid for it by renting the top two levels to two other Irish families.

When I get to the middle door of the apartments which had been converted to one large apartment, I knock on the door. They had chosen this as the main entrance because it leads directly into the kitchen of the second apartment, which is the central hub of the O'Shea family comings and goings.

"Come in!" my Mum calls at the door. The O'Shea residence has had an open-door policy for as long as I can remember. Whenever someone shows up at the door, they are always invited in, no questions asked, and made to feel welcome. I open the door and step into the kitchen which smells deliciously like the traditional Irish soda bread and lamb stew. "Colin!" she cries from near the stove.

"Hi Mum!" I say brightly, my spirits instantly lifted at seeing her plump, red face.

Per usual, she's covered in flour and wearing her kitchen apron which sports the holly leaves of the upcoming holiday on it. She's got an apron for every holiday and she rotates them accordingly.

"Still wearing those ratty old things," I tease her as I hug her. She's soft and warm and even though I am a grown man, I hold on for just a second longer, needing the hug from my Mum. She doesn't ask what's wrong, that would be too direct for her Christian upbringing. Instead she says, "Now don't start with me about the aprons. They save my clothes from being ruined by feeding all of you!"

"How many times do I have to tell you to come up to the city and I'll take you on a proper shopping trip, so you don't look like a dowdy soccer mom?" I explain patiently.

She whacks my shoulder with the spatula she is holding.

"Oh, that would be the day, wouldn't it? There's nothing wrong with soccer, mind you. Our Kathy just tried out for the varsity team this year and made left wing, she did."

"That's excellent!" I say, meaning it. If it's one thing my Mum will always boast about, it is the accomplishment of her kids. She'll never say a word about herself or her appearance whether good or bad, but she will always take pride in us.

"That's right. So never you mind about me looking like a soccer Mum," she chides as she turns back to the stove.

She lifts the lid off the pot and stirs the stew. It has always been one of my favorites and the savory smell that wafts through the room makes me glad to be home. I look around and take in the kitchen. It hasn't changed at all with its peeling yellow sunflower wall paper and shelves crammed with pots and pans and food stuffs. The fridge is plastered in old report cards, drawings and finger paints. The most current being from her new pride and joy, Liam's son, Aiden. Aiden is the first grandchild and the apple of Mum's eye.

He totters into the kitchen in nothing but a diaper, t-shirt and pacifier. He holds his arms up when he sees me, and I oblige, hoisting the little tyke onto my hip as I dance with him around the kitchen. He laughs as my Mum watches us and rolls out cinnamon rolls on the counter for dessert.

As I play with Aiden, she fills me in on the rest of the family's news and drama and I listen and take notes for the upcoming holiday break. I don't want to step on any toes and occasionally, when there's too much Bushmills involved with the celebrations, things can get heated quickly. It's best not to offend Sarah's new boyfriend by getting the name of his pet Pitbull wrong or some such nonsense like that.

Mum remains stalwart in not asking outright what's wrong, but she skirts the question by asking about school. I tell her of the upcoming performances and about Katarina's being on the fence about drama or dancing. She had taken an instant liking to Katarina when I brought her home last Thanksgiving to celebrate with us. She had, according to

Katarina, pulled her into the kitchen and thanked her for being such an understanding best friend who was there for me to confide in about what she deemed, "life and love things."

After that conversation, Mum deemed it prudent to consider Katarina as one of her own, and Katarina willingly went into the family fold, as her own parents are still in Russia, and they rarely had time for her anyway, being social and political figureheads. It's still questionable if my Dad and brothers think she was my "cure" but one look from my Mum told them all to shut up about it and not ask such a question.

Just as I am about to get to the part of the kiss and the drama that unfolded with that, she pauses in her stirring and says, "A Mum knows. I made your favorite tonight because, somehow, I just knew."

"You're a psychic now, Mum?" I tease. "I never called so how did you predict I'd be coming home tonight? Especially seeing as it's a weekday night."

"Don't be silly, Colin O'Shea, you know I don't hold with that willy nilly hocus pocus nonsense. A Mum just knows when one of her babies is coming around because they need her. That's why I made your favorite tonight, weekday or not." She nods her head in affirmation and turns back to the pot as I roll my eyes heavenward.

For a Christian woman, she has some insights into things that can only be described as a divine connection to higher powers. It might just be that connection that gives her a direct line to the Lord Almighty, as she calls him, or her uncanny ability to just "know things." I've long since made my peace with my religious upbringing and the fact that because of my preferences, I am shunned at large in that community. There are those in this age, like Mum, who say that the Lord loves us anyway, but I am well aware of the discrimination. I will always remain respectful of that upbringing, even if it is solely for her benefit. I'm kind of glad she has these premonitions, so to speak, because I realize I've been smiling since I walked in the door and received my hug. Something I hadn't been doing at Julliard, and something that is momentarily disrupted when my Dad and brothers walk through the door and see me sitting at the kitchen table with Aiden and Mum.

"Colin. This is a surprise," Dad says quietly. I stand and shake his hand. Seamus and Liam give me a pat on the back with a quick hug and tousle my hair like when we were kids. Liam scoops up Aiden who laughs gleefully in his arms as he greets his Dad. I say hello to Patrick who shoves his hands in his pockets. He had once been drunk and told me not to touch him so "it" wouldn't rub off on him. We keep a respectful distance from one another now.

"Hello, Dad. I hope you don't mind me stopping in tonight," I say. I search his face which has gone instantly passive, but he nods his head.

"Not at all. You'll be staying for dinner of course." It isn't a question, more a statement and I nod.

"Ah, yes, Sir. Thank you for having me."

Mum tsks at him as she gives him a kiss hello. "Of course, he's staying for dinner, Finn. The boy is skin and bones."

"Of course," Dad reiterates. "Will you be staying over as well? I need to clear a few boxes from your room if that's the case."

"Um, no. I wasn't planning on it. I have classes tomorrow. I just…I wanted to come home tonight and see everyone," I finish lamely. No one here really wants to speak openly about whatever reason I have come home, so offering a ready-made excuse is a good way to bypass that awkwardness.

Kathy, Sarah, and Collene enter the kitchen and begin grabbing dishes to set the table. They had come in to greet me when I got there. The room's tension almost visibly lessens as they learn I won't be staying over, and the thought makes me momentarily sad. Sometimes I get angry that they are so uncomfortable around me, like they are on edge, and sometimes I understand why and can't blame them.

Dinner passes relatively normally for an O'Shea gathering. Mum is glowing because she has all her children around the table. None of us dare disrupt her reverie and happiness by having the audacity to fight or argue, and as I observe Dad and the increased silver in his auburn hair, I notice even he seems more relaxed and content than usual.

I say my goodbyes and Mum makes me promise to bring Katarina for Christmas before I head back to the train station. Mum pulls me aside and makes me promise to send tickets for the performance. She has been to a couple and I am hoping she will convince Dad to come see one. He hasn't been up to the school yet to see me, and I am not holding my breath that she can convince him to bring her up for Valentine's Day. Dad makes the offer to drive me, but I know he will be up at three am to head to the docks for work again, so I thank him, but pull my hoodie back on, obscuring my face and blending in with the pedestrians to get to the station.

Parts of Southie can be dangerous at night, but if you look as shady as some of the seedier areas, you can blend in and no one will harass you. I make it all the way to the train station unmolested and purchase my ticket back to the city. When I get on the train and go to pull my headphones on to drown out the noise, I look across the aisle, and do a double take when I see Gregor sitting in the seat opposite me, staring at me with rapture. I had no idea he came from Boston, and judging by the look on his face, neither did he regarding me. We both start laughing nervously as he moves across the aisle and sits next to me for the trip. It's uncanny how fate brought us to the point that we both decided an emergency trip home was just what was necessary for our souls.

CHAPTER SIX

"*I* didn't know you are from Boston," I blurt out, stating the obvious.

"Yeah, my Mom moved there from Philly when I was six. It's just me, my siblings, and her," he tells me. I don't ask about his Dad. There's no need to. He has that tone when he says his Mom that suggests she has been Mom, Dad, and any variation of guidance or friend he has needed through the years.

"How many siblings do you have?" I ask casually.

"There's me, Joey, Tanya, and then Shea."

"You have a big family too," I state. He looks at me and then nods in agreement.

"I wasn't sure if you came from a big Irish family, I didn't want to assume."

I appreciate his candor. "So, home to visit on a school night, huh?" I ask.

He quirks an eyebrow at me as if to suggest, "Yeah? You too, I see."

I bite my lip and look out the train window. It's dark outside and I can't see the city scape as we pass through and head north to New York. I can see his reflection in the pane of glass. The lights had been dimmed on the train to allow for overnight travelers since it is the late train. Classes are going to be rough again tomorrow, but home was just where I needed to be tonight.

Gregor is leaning back in his seat, his legs slightly parted and arm thrown over the back of the seat. I am acutely aware of his hand near the side of my head and I want nothing more than to turn to him and lean against his chest like the couple in the seat in front of us is doing.

I fish around in my brain, wondering what else other than the performance I should talk to him about. When I look back at him, his eyes are hooded, as the light is shining from behind him, but he is definitely watching me.

"Ahh…" I start but he cuts me off.

"I'm sorry for the position I put you in last night," he whispers so as not to disturb anyone around us.

"It's ok. Eric has the uncanny ability to be the center of attention for anything. So I'm sure being the one to walk in on something like that was just the kind of attention that he needed when he spread it all over school," I gripe.

Gregor chuckles and his white teeth flash in the darkness. I watch his lips as his laughter fades and his brow is then drawn into a frown.

"You want me to say something to him?" he asks. There's a

hint of malice in his tone, like he has suddenly become fiercely protective of me. I shy away from him and start to shut down immediately.

"No, it's fine. I mean, it was just a kiss, right? Nothing that won't blow over in a couple of days. I mean, I'm sure you have other stuff to focus on, like the audition and everything. At least, that's what I am working on this week. So, it's best not to let, ah, other stuff get in the way."

He raises an eyebrow and suddenly I feel like I might have offended him.

"Sorry. I didn't mean to upset you. It's just, I hope you realize that's my focus at school." I chew my lip nervously as the intensity of his gaze bores into mine.

"I think," he starts slowly, "it would be a mistake to say that was just a simple kiss. There was nothing simple about it. Don't you agree?"

I open my mouth to argue, but there really is no point. To deny it would be a lie, and we both know it. Instead, I try to change the subject, thereby switching my aversion tactics.

"How did you get into Julliard? What made you want to be an actor?" I ask.

A long pause ensues before he answers. He plays along with my avoidance game.

"I always wanted to be an actor. I was in the drama club when I was in high school. I had a great mentor and teacher who knows Mr. Schlewp. He came to see Dreamgirls. I played Curtis Taylor Jr., the shady business dealer of the singer trio."

I nod, impressed that his high school had taken on such a well-known piece.

"Mr. Schlewp loved the performance and came to the high school to talk to me and Mr. Friedman about my future after school. Julliard offered me a scholarship, and I also do the work study program, working with Julliard to screen high schools around the city to look for new talent."

"Wow, that's impressive!" I tell him. He must be pretty impressive to get taken on by Julliard after just having graduated.

"Thanks. I love it at the school. Of course, Mom is always telling people I'm going to be a big movie star."

"Don't all Moms want what's best for their kids?" I ask.

"Yeah, something like that. What about your Mom?" he inquires.

"My Mum is really supportive. She always has been, about… everything." He taps his chin thoughtfully.

"Sounds like you have it all figured out then," he says. I shrug.

"I guess so."

"So tell me then, where and when does that leave time for you?"

I look at him, confused.

"What do you mean?"

"Just that, you have dance, and you have your family, and Katrina is cool if not a bit confused about what she wants, I just wonder when you have time to for you. You know, other friends, socializing, dating…" With the last word he trails off and waits for a response, successfully bringing my previous topic of conversation back around full circle.

"I, ah, don't really date." I inform him.

"Yeah, I get that, but why not?"

"Well, like you said, there's school and dancing. That is what is important to me."

"I think you are hiding from the socializing and dating, because it's easier for you to not deal."

I blink at him. His blunt honesty hits home. "I don't know that it's really your concern," I tell him politely. I can feel my heart beat faster as he smiles at me.

"It wasn't meant to offend you. Just that I have a vested interest in you."

"Really?" I snicker. "How so?"

"Well, I'm interested, and when I go after someone who captures my interest, I tend to invest a lot of time and energy into them." He jokes with me.

"Yeah, I got that the other night," I murmur, looking at his lips again. I think about everything that has happened in the last twenty-four hours and how much it has thrown me off kilter. "Gregor, it's just, I am really dedicated to my dancing. I don't know if I have enough time to get into a serious relationship," I tell him honestly.

"How are you going to know if you don't give me a chance?" He sits up, leaning toward me. The intensity of his gaze leaves me feeling trapped in the corner seat. I have no way out of this. There is no way I can avoid not answering his question. "Katarina told me you don't date. How you avoid having a boyfriend."

"Well, she shouldn't have. It's none of her business really."

"Maybe. But she did. And I think you avoid having relationships because you're afraid of getting hurt. But I think if you give me a chance you'll find I can prove you wrong. I won't be a distraction from your dancing. I'll be supportive. I think that will shine through in the spirit of your dancing," he argues his point further.

I bite my lip, not really sure if I'm ready to make this jump yet. But with him here, right now, it is impossible not to lean into him and inhale his intoxicating scent. He answers my gesture by letting his arm that was on the back of the seat fall down and wrap around me, pulling me closer and pressing me to him. He initiates the kiss, even though I moved toward him, and in the soft light of the train, I get lost in his arms as we sit there kissing and whispering to each other all the way back to Grand Central Station.

When the train pulls to a stop, I see in his face that he is reluctantly letting go of me as he stands and begins filing out of the car. I follow him and when he hops down onto the platform, he waits for me and links his hand with mine as we begin the walk back to the school.

It's late and I yawn as we walk through the city, taking in the night life and viewing all of the lights that surround us.

"Are you headed to bed when we get back?" he asks me suddenly.

"Yeah probably. I have a five am class in the morning." I say through another yawn.

"Well, it's almost two in the morning now. When was the last time you pulled an all nighter?" He looks down at me with a mischievous grin on his face.

"Umm, a long time from never." I admit laughing at him. "I'm not staying up all night. I'd never make it through classes," I tell him.

"Sure, you will. That's one thing I admire about you," he confesses.

"Really? How do you know?"

He shrugs. "Just from what Katarina has told me. And I've watched you dance before," he admits.

"I'm not sure which part of that statement I should start with." I chuckle. "Katarina has a big mouth and I'm going to tape it shut, to start." He laughs at this. "And, you watch me dance?"

He shrugs again but nods, sitting on a bench a few blocks from school and pulling me down next to him. "Sure, I do. You first caught my attention last year. When you and Katarina were in the solarium at the atrium of the school. You were horsing around and dancing with each other. It's one of the rare times I've seen you smile."

I crack a grin at this, remembering the day he was talking about. We were new to the school and drunk on the euphoria of having been admitted to such a prestigious school. It was only a few weeks after we had met and become fast friends, before I had been given a hard time by Madame so much and decided fun was out of the question at Julliard. My smile fades with that thought. I had spent the rest of the year busting my butt trying to get in shape to be good enough, and days like that had come fewer and farther in between.

"Yeah I remember that day. I knew people were probably watching us and thinking we were crazy, showing off or just young and naïve." I admit.

"Nah, not to me. You were being true." He pulls me closer to him, a gesture that feels so strange to me. We sit another few moments and watch the city pass us by. "You ever seen those dancing movies, you know, 'Save the Last Dance' or 'Center Stage'? What about 'Dirty Dancing'?" He asks excitedly.

"Yeah of course. Why?" He jumps up with a mixed look of joy and mischief again.

"Because, you remind me of those movies when you dance just to have fun," he tells me.

"Alright, but what's your point?" I wonder.

"That's what you need for your audition!" His idea suddenly begins to dawn on me. In all of those movies, the dancers were the underdogs who rose up and let their passion shine through their dancing. In "Save the Last Dance" the characters faced adversity for being a bi-racial couple, just like in Rent. The characters face adversity for being HIV positive and for having alternative lifestyles.

"I could do that!" I suddenly jump up with him, my excitement renewed. "I could choreograph something like that!"

He nods in agreement. "Come on, I have an idea."

We rush back to the school and up the stairs. I think we are going to stop and watch movies for the rest of the evening or something. Just as some way to get us pumped up for his idea, but we keep traveling upward in the building. We climb the stairs to the very last landing, and Gregor takes a chain out from under his shirt and unlocks a gray, nondescript door at the end of a bare hallway.

When we step out of the door, the predawn breeze hits my body and cools me from the exertion of running up the steps, and I see that we are now out on the gravel top roof.

"How did you get roof access?" I ask him.

"Mr. Schlewp gave me a key last year to come up and practice lines and stuff," he tells me.

"This is incredible. It's like being able to reach out and touch the whole city." I look around in wonder. The city scape is eye level with us now, and the millions of lights shine brightly in the darkness like twinkling stars. I walk over to the ledge of the roof and look down. Hundreds of feet below us, the hustle and bustle of the city continues. Even in the early morning hours, traffic is almost as heavy as a normal, busy working day.

All thoughts of fatigue, stress, and worry leave me as I marvel at the different viewpoints of the city. I look back at Gregor and see him in a new light too. I had seriously misjudged him. He was trying to show me that we come from similar places and have similar goals all along. I feel a twinge of emotion in my chest I've been afraid to allow myself to feel. He had recognized whatever this is, in me, last year when he saw me dancing. I guess he has just been biding his time until it was right to approach me.

"Did you get close to Katarina to be able to introduce yourself to me?" I ask. I startle even myself with the bluntness of the question.

"Fifty-fifty," he confesses. "She really is a cool chick and I think I almost have her convinced to switch to the dark side." He laughs.

"Drama is the dark side now?" I raise an eyebrow. I never pegged him for the Star Wars geek-out type, but then again, he is showing me layers tonight.

"Yeah, comedy and tragedy." He laughs. "It's a tragedy we didn't get her when she first started at Julliard."

I laugh along with him then look at the wide expanse of the rooftop.

"This is incredible. I can't believe your good fortune for having access to such a place."

I give the surface a twirl and laugh when gravel sprays up from under my heel. Gregor watches me as he leans back against the rooftop concrete railing. He fishes his phone out of his pocket and hits speaker. He queues up a remix of the song, "I See Your True Colors" from the movie, "Save The Last Dance" and I let the music take me as I dance around the rooftop. I've never been the best at hip hop, but as I pass by him one more time, he sweeps in and begins dancing with me. We move like I have envisioned Angela and Eric move, mostly in large sweeping motions and circles around the roof. He twirls me as I pirouette, and he even does a dip as the music switches to "I've Had the Time of My Life" from "Dirty Dancing."

We move through all the songs on what I have dubbed, "Dance List" on my own phone. And I let myself get lost in the music and in him as we move.

We break around dawn and watch the sun come up, and when he sees me shivering in fatigue and emotion, he draws me into his chest again as he holds me.

It all feels a bit surreal, or maybe that's how tired I am, but I allow myself to be captured and pulled back into his arms as we watch the sun surface over the city skyline.

"We better get you to class," he murmurs after a while. His

body radiates heat and I had almost fallen asleep as I leaned against him and the rail.

I tilt my head back, wondering how much I am going to let myself fall before reality and the need to continue being motivated in school, force me to pull away from him. As I lean up for another kiss before we go, all that stress flies off the rooftop on the early morning breeze.

CHAPTER SEVEN

I don't really feel the effects of pulling the all nighter until lunch time. Madame Roussou hadn't found a single thing to comment on my form all through the morning class. Even Eric and Angela's snickers went by unnoticed as I danced to find the feeling I had on the rooftop.

Katarina catches up with me after class as we head to the dining hall, and starts harassing me with questions.

"What has gotten into you?" she asks.

"What do you mean?" I whistle the tune from the "Dirty Dancing: Havana Nights" movie.

"You look like shit and yet you're on cloud nine today!" she exclaims.

"Oh yeah, I guess I am!" I tell her happily, grabbing a water from the cooler by the registers. I check out and head to our usual table. When I get halfway there I stop. "Hey, do you

60

want to see if maybe the drama kids will let us sit with them?" I ask her.

"Are you on drugs?" she blurts out.

"What?" I look at her, confused.

"You show up to class with black circles under your eyes that make a junkie look refreshed. Then you go on to outshine Eric and Angela, to the point Madame couldn't find one single thing to say badly about your form. You must be on some sort of high," she finishes.

I look around. No one has heard her blurt that out, because if they had, I would be taking a steroid test so quickly it would make my head spin. Julliard has a strict policy on drugs or steroids of any kind.

"Katarina, are you nuts? Don't say something like that out loud for the wolves to hear. No, I'm not. To answer your question, I'm just in a really good mood. I went home and saw my Mum last night, which by the way, she wants you to come for Christmas this year. And then I had an amazing evening hanging out with…" I realize what I am about to confess to her.

"Who? With who?" She jumps up and down excitedly.

"With Gregor," I finish. She squeals as she hops in a motion that resembles an assemble.

"You and Gregor?" she breaths.

"Yes, and I'm pretty sure I have you to thank for that." I raise my eyebrows at her. "Gregor was very enlightening about how he came to be so interested in me in the first place. I think there's a certain best friend I have to thank, or maybe yell at, I'm not sure which."

She punches me lightly on the arm. "Thank God!" she breathes out. "Do you have any idea how much work it has been to get you to open up your eyes and notice him?"

I scowl at her then grin. "You're a pest. Go away, Katarina."

"Not a chance. Now that I've got the two of you speaking to each other, and kissing, we need to go on to step two of the dating game for you."

"Katarina," I warn. "this is new to me. And I already told Gregor, I do not want it interfering with my dancing, and he assured me he would be respectful of that."

She sighs and flips her braid over her shoulder. "You're such hard work sometimes, Colin," she gripes. I laugh and tug her braid behind her head, then look toward the drama table. I was hoping Gregor would be there, but I don't see him yet.

"Well, he isn't there so maybe we should just..." I trail off. He has just entered the dining hall and he looks around, spots me and smiles. I smile back, but it is a grimace, as I see Seth is with him and chatting his ear off. "Let's just go sit at our usual table. He looks busy." I turn to head to our corner, but Katarina pushes on my side.

"Oh no you don't. Move your butt, Irish. You want Gregor, go stake a claim and put yourself between him and Seth. Besides, there are other people I want to introduce you to who are cool in the drama program." She pushes me toward the table and I reluctantly walk over on my own, so she won't embarrass me. When we get there, the whole table goes quiet as they stare at us holding our trays in nothing but tights, unitards, and sweatshirts against the chill. I suddenly feel very awkward and exposed and wonder what the hell I was thinking in believing this was a good idea. All at once my fatigue comes crashing down around me and I want to slouch out of the dining hall and sink down into my bed like a slug and hide until everyone forgets my name.

"Hey, Katarina!" A blond girl with green eyes wearing a cat costume calls to us. "Who's your friend?" she asks. No one bats an eye at her with her painted-on whiskers and for a fleeting moment, I feel like out of the ordinary might be the norm for this group. I suddenly feel a palm on my shoulder and recognize the searing heat from Gregor's touch.

"This is Colin. He's with me," he tells his friends. All at once they break out into normal chatter, moving their seats over and letting us squeeze into the table which is already over-crowded by at least ten people. I listen in to the flow of their conversation, it's a blend of street talk mixed with theatrical references and pop culture. I begin to get the flow of things as they introduce themselves. I will never be able to remember all their names, but I am pretty good with faces as they make me feel welcome. I look over at Katarina, who is smiling at me, and then she looks pointedly down at my lap. Gregor had linked his fingers with my own and no one has said a thing about it one way or another. The only one who seemed to take issue with my presence was Seth, who spent the remainder of lunch sitting directly behind us, causing us to lean apart as he would lean in and chat with Gregor. He was intentionally splitting us apart, physically separating us so he could lean right in to whisper in Gregor's ear. It seemed rude of me to keep my back turned to him the entire meal, despite the fact that he wasn't including me in any of his conversations with Gregor.

After lunch, Katarina glared at Seth's retreating back and gave me a peck on the cheek. "Catch up with me in class?" I nodded as I dropped my tray off at the dishes collection area and walked out into the hall with Gregor. His group of friends was waiting for him down the hall some ways, and I noticed Seth glowering at us as Gregor turned me to him.

"Same place after dinner?" he asked hopefully. I felt nervous as other people stared at us. This was exactly the kind of attention I didn't want. As if sensing my apprehension, he added, "It will just be us. We can work on some moves for the choreographed piece if you want, or just hang out. You look pretty tired." He brushed my cheek with his thumb. I felt so torn wanting to be alone with him again, but hating that I felt like a freak show as other people watched us have a private moment.

"Yeah, I'll head up there after class," I told him. I leaned in and gave him an awkward hug by patting him on the back like a child. I heard snickers behind me as I turned away and dashed down the hall after Katarina who was rolling her eyes at me. I didn't dare turn around to see the look on his face, afraid I'd run and hide in my room from mortification for petting him like he was some kind of animal. Instead I hang my head as we trudge to class, and hold up a hand as she starts to say something. "Just, please don't," I whisper as we enter the room and sit on the benches to pull on our shoes.

I powder my shoes and head to the barre to start stretching. The feeling of elation is completely deflated, as Madame spends the entire class, critiquing my overly rigid posture. I try to relax a little and internally curse myself for getting so caught up in the whirlwind of last night. I make a vow to myself to tell Gregor when I get on the roof this afternoon that we need to cool it. What really irks me is the sneers on Eric and Angela's face as I go to lift Katarina that afternoon, and physically and mentally exhausted, I drop her so that we both land in a heap on the floor.

I quickly get up and pick her up, checking to make sure she

isn't injured, and I then turn to the coldly disapproving stare of Madame.

"I don't know what you ate at lunch today, O'Shea, but the lack of discipline you are showing in this afternoon's class has me wondering if you are truly taking your dancing career seriously or not. This school is built to house and train the best dancers, not the ones who show up with part time attention and focus. If you ever think to land a primo role, you need to demonstrate more self-discipline and dedication to the craft than what I have just witnessed. Your friend Katarina may be toying with the idea of switching programs, but you do not have such a luxury as you are here on a dance scholarship only." She turns and walks away down the line of ballerinas who are completely silent as they stare at us.

I feel my cheeks burn with humiliation as I mouth an apology to Katarina once more. Her eyes are blank and cold as they stare after Madame. I have a good idea where she got the information about Katarina's decision to switch programs, but there is no way to prove it. Katarina turns that hauntingly chilling gaze from Madame onto Eric and Angela, whose faces are cracked with laughter. They falter when they see the look in her eyes. Her anger even scares me a little. I turn my attention back to the barre where I stretch out and then gesture for Katarina to try the lift again. Madame doesn't say another word to us for the entire class. I am almost grateful if it weren't for the fact that her criticisms had been a sign that she cares.

When class is over, I run out of the room and race up the stairs to the top landing. The door is already unlocked, and I land on the gravel with a light bounce as I stare at Gregor's back.

"We can't see each other. I knew it was a mistake. I was distracted and I dropped Katarina in class. Madame called her out for wanting to switch programs and it's all too distracting," I blurt out in one breath.

Gregor turns around looking gorgeous in a white tank top and jeans. The late afternoon sun is warm and there is a sheen of sweat on his muscled chest. "So that's it then? One bad experience and you're ready to throw in the towel and call it quits?" he asks.

"Yes. Yes, I am. This won't work," I insist.

"Ok then. I'll give up on one condition," he tells me. I look at him, completely perplexed.

"What is it?"

He hits play on the music app on his phone, and the song "Warriors" from Michael Flatley's "Lord of the Dance" begins. I know this song. I'm so familiar with it from my performance. It is a battle of wills. Light and dark. Anger and happiness.

"Dance with me," Gregor tells me.

"Huh?" I feel the tempo kick into something dark and beautiful. It's as if the eroticism from the music takes form in the shape of Gregor as he stalks toward me.

"I said, dance with me. Dance out your anger and then try talking to me again. If you still feel like we won't work out after we dance, then I will back off. No questions asked. I'll give you space and boundaries that I won't push. But dance your stress out like you did last night," he says. I am about to protest at the absurdity of his request, but then I remember this is my life. Dancing. And I let him sweep me into the music and a twirl with the tempo. Gregor isn't a world-renowned tap dancer, but he is able to spin and circle with me to the beat of the music. His footwork isn't fancy, and occasionally he backs off, watching as I allow the memory of the steps to fill my mind and I spin off into a segment of the dance I recall from my performance. But by the end of the music, he has captured me again and we are twirling in circles on the rooftop. Gravel sprays up under our sneakers and sweat is dripping down off us as we move. But when the music stops, I have a singular moment of confusion as to all the arguments that surfaced in my head that I was going to point out that were the reasons seeing each other is a bad idea; then I realize I can't remember a single one.

I hop onto him then. He steps back, catching me. He's twice my size and taller than me, so I feel his arms bunch as he hoists me up and I wrap my legs around his waist. He leans back against an air duct concrete block and then we are kissing each other. I forget about the afternoon session. I forget about Katarina's stunned, hurt, and angry face. And I forget about Madame's harsh words and Eric's smug look. I curse myself internally as I come to realize there are some things worth dancing for, and Gregor McCallum happens to fall under my list of worth dancing for, and that isn't going to change any time soon.

CHAPTER EIGHT

*T*he following few days are spent in grueling sessions and much the same way as the first day with Gregor had. We'd met on the rooftop and choreographed a piece together. Part of the rules of the audition were, we could dance with one another and do a joint piece, but we would be judged based on singular performance, as well as a pair. So that could potentially hurt or hinder my chances. Gregor isn't a bad dancer. He is definitely more of a free stylist, but we use that to our advantage when we create the piece. He helps me through some of the readings, as he tells me occasionally my acting voice is flat and emotionless.

"I have a hard time feeling these characters," I confess. "I portray characters through my body," I explain.

"Well it's the same in drama, just a different form," he counters. "In drama, you become that person. You can't tell me there is nothing that is similar in these characters on paper as in your own life?" he asks.

I look at the lines and read the characters again. "Well, no. I know the piece is designed to be eclectic and different, but I'm not a professor or HIV positive. I know there is a stigmatism with being gay and people automatically assume I am. But other than being gay…"

"Think Colin. White guy in love with a black guy. Both have AIDS. Several of these characters are struggling artists, facing adversity. You may not be a drag queen but there is definitely some discrimination in your life for being a cross-dresser."

"What? What are you talking about?" I demand. He's chuckling so I know he didn't say it to be offensive, he's just pulling my leg.

"You wear a leotard," he states simply.

I look down at my tights and unitard. "It's the class dress code!" I tell him indignantly. He holds up his hands, laughing outright as I whack him with my script.

We're on the roof again, this having become our spot to practice. It's almost dusk and the heat of the day is beginning to cool, and so with it, our bodies from the perspiration of dancing.

"Whatever you say man," he chuckles, and I grin.

"I don't get on your case about being from the hood or wearing baggy jeans and stuff," I insist. He laughs again.

He had explained his dad was some rich board member who had met his mom in Philadelphia, where she was studying to become a lawyer. She got pregnant with him and his dad convinced her to move in with him, where they had three more children. When he hit his mid-life crisis, he decided the pressure he received for being in a bi-racial relationship was too much, and he traded Gregor's mom for a young, skinny blonde woman who had just entered the university and was giving her a leg up in the firm so to speak. They had moved to Boston after his mom walked in on his dad and the paralegal discussing their next "case" after hours.

She had settled in Boston, working her way through the ranks of a local firm, working pro bono and long hours to feed her kids. She never looked back.

He had a point, though. Even in the age of enlightenment, the discrimination that is faced is evident everywhere. The musical is going to be a breaking piece for the school as it embraces the diversity of its students.

I look at the characters with a new light, and put as much of my own emotion as I can in the reading. When we are done, Gregor snaps the script shut and pulls me into a hug.

"That was perfect!" he exclaims. "I think we're finally ready for tomorrow!"

It's the night before auditions, and Madame had done a rare thing, and given us the day off of classes. I had immediately made my way here with Gregor. We had worked ourselves to exhaustion, until we went down for dinner, then came back up to do the readings. I had wanted to do the readings someplace comfier, like in one of our dorms, but Gregor had insisted the readings were as integral as the dancing, and we needed to be on our toes and on edge.

When he pulls away, I feel every last bit of energy drain from my body, physically and mentally. I have nothing more to give until the next day when the audition would happen. Gregor looks as equally exhausted as he has been working just as hard on the dancing to get the moves just right.

"What now?" I ask him wearily as I lean against the concrete base of the air duct. My muscles are so sore I don't know if I am going to be able to move to climb down all those flights of stairs in order to collapse into bed.

"It just so happens, I anticipated this moment," he says. He rubs his eyes as he tries to wake himself up a little and hoists himself up. He goes around one of the big ventilation fans and brings back a duffel bag, which is packed full of something.

"What on earth is all that?" I ask, moving away from the concrete block as he sets the bag down in the middle of the roof.

"Our reward and respite," he explains. He pulls a blanket out and spreads it over the gravel. It is soft and cushions the gritty feeling under us as we sit down on it. Before too long, I am too tired to keep my body upright, and allow myself to drift down and gaze up at the stars as they begin to make their way up shining through the city lights. They are very dim, but from way up here they are noticeable; if we were on the ground level, we wouldn't be able to see them through the smog.

Gregor lays down next to me and I tuck my head on the crook of his arm as he pulls his arms above his head. He smells like gravel and sweat, but my senses are too fatigued to notice if I really care.

Before too long, he is kissing me again and I feel something break inside me. Some resistance to him that I have been keeping in check. I realize there is something to be said for a man who is willing to throw caution to the wind and take a chance on a man and see him through an audition that could make or break both of their careers. I realize, without understanding what I want from him, that I still want something else.

I deepen the kiss this time, becoming more ferocious and nipping at his full bottom lip in earnest. I lean up over him and let my kisses explore his jaw and neck. I have never done this to a man and I occasionally pause to watch his face to see if what I am doing is okay, but the look of lust he has in his eyes tells me if I stop now, he won't let me escape fast enough to pull away from him.

I let my kisses trail down his dark chest, and when I get to the tank top, his muscles bunch as he sits up and whips it over his head. I have no idea where our renewed sense of vigor and energy is coming from. Maybe it's urgency for tomorrow, but I continue my exploration down his chest, stopping as I reach his dark nipples. I suck one into my mouth and he lets out a low groan as his body contorts under me and his hands find the back of my head. He applies light pressure as he pushes me down and I let my tongue taste the saltiness of his skin as I trace a path down his hard abdomen. I nip him just under his navel where the small crease of skin bunches, and his breath quickens as I pause over his zipper.

"I've never done this," I whisper up at him.

"Have you ever had it done to you?" I shake my head.

"Ah, a girl tried in high school, but I wasn't…I didn't…" I trail off. No need to go down that memory lane. I had known for a while, but like some naïve guys who are in denial, I thought I could try things with a girl and somehow be cured. It had ended badly for both of us, and I cringe internally at the way things ended that night. I feel bad for her now and hope she found someone to make her happy. She wasn't cruel but there was some definite awkwardness.

Gregor shudders underneath me. "Nothing? Ever? I'm the first?" he asks.

"Um, yeah. I've kissed a few guys but…" I let my confession hang in the air, wondering if he is going to make me stop. His hand reaches down, and he snaps the button on his jeans.

"I'll guide you through it," he whispers down at me in the darkness. He has leaned up, so his free arm is perched on the blanket and he is able to look down at me, kneeling between his thighs now. His muscles twitch, even that much I can see in the light of the city buildings around us. I wonder vaguely if we can be seen from any building, but as I can't make out any figures in windows, I gauge we are a safe enough distance away from people that we won't be caught for indecent exposure.

He lifts his hips, freeing himself from the confines of his jeans, and the length of him springs free, hard and ready. I gulp, taking in the size of him. He isn't huge like I've seen on internet videos. I'll admit it, I've looked. Since I didn't have a man in my life, it was the only place I could explore to see what I like. He is hard and ready though. I get what I'm supposed to do next and I bend my head over him as he cups the back of my head. He doesn't force me down on him as I expected from those videos, but lets me explore on my own.

The first touch with the tip of my tongue has his hips jack knife up off the blanket. I don't know what I was expecting, but seeing the look of pure bliss as I close my lips around the head of him is enough to know that I like this feeling. Like I am in charge. I have the power here even though he is bigger than me. If I were to rate the level of manliness, I guess I could call it, I would definitely say he is more masculine, although I don't see myself as gay and effeminate. He groans as I explore with my tongue and mouth. I seal my lips around him and mimic the motions of up and down that I had seen on the videos. I discover there are certain things he likes and he encourages me with moans and soft whispers when I do them and there are things that he lets his head fall back and just enjoy the feel of, although it isn't anything to push him over the edge yet.

One of the things I discover, he enjoys the flick of my tongue over the tip of him, and it causes him to jerk and groan when I do it. My mouth feels full of him as I explore, and I begin to wonder what will happen if I do it to him over and over. I squirm on the blanket, trying to find a comfortable way to lay where my length is pressed to the blanket and hard concrete roof. The pressure is uncomfortable, and I finally settle on leaning up on my knees so that it's not pressed against anything but my tights, which I suddenly realize are the bane of my existence. Seeing and feeling his reactions of helplessness where I take charge, as he had been the one to take charge all week, have me throbbing in my tights.

His hands clench in the blanket below him as I start to flick my tongue over the tip of him. He raises his hips, almost in motion that begs for more contact, but I hold it back. He catches on quickly to what I am doing, and he only permits me to do this to him a couple of times more, before his ability to maintain self-control is tested.

He sits up and whips me around, so I am now the one lying supine on the blanket. He wastes no time working his way down, nipping my hips through my tights with his teeth. The shock of the feeling sends jolts of pleasure through my body, landing in between my thighs, and I suddenly understand the dance he had been doing with his own hips. The intensity is too much. I look down the length of his torso and see him swaying, hanging low and heavy between his thighs. I desperately want nothing more than to be back in control, pleasing him with my mouth. But I have pushed him past the point of no return. He has taken the lead once again, just like when we are dancing, and I bite the back of my hand to keep from shouting out when I feel his hot breath and warm wet mouth make contact with me, teasing me through the tights.

He's merciless as he works down the length of me. The friction isn't enough, and he knows it. He sits back on his heels after a few moments of torment, and croakily says, "Don't all dancers require a warm up? Now you know how this goes…"

He breaks off his sentence as he watches my trembling fingers reach between us and cup him. He closes his eyes as he shudders, but opens them when he feels my other hand reach down subconsciously as I try to cup and squeeze myself to find relief.

"Not yet," he commands, grasping my wrist and holding it away.

"Gregor, please!" I gasp, needing some sort of friction. I can feel my hips squirming under him as he denies me what I need, just as I denied him. We are feeding from each other, only this is a dance I don't recognize and he's the leader.

He lets go of my wrist and places my palm against the blanket at my side. My fingers curl instinctively finding something to hold on to. I feel his own hands at the waistband of my tights and I lift my hips as he rolls them down.

Shock slams into my system as the heat and relief I feel exit my body, only to be greeted with the cool night air, mixed with the warm puffs of his breath. I clench my teeth so hard my jaw aches. I want to beg him to touch me, or do the things I did to him, but my brain snaps my mouth shut, unsure of how to ask.

He blows on the tip of me and I try to sit up. Oh dear God! It's too much, but with a firm hand, he pushes me back down. I feel my hands move from the blanket to the back of his curly head, and my fingers snare in his hair.

When the touch of his tongue runs up the underside of the tip of me, it's so sensitive that I jerk under him, trying to squirm out of his reach. He parts his mouth over the top of me, trapping me under him, and my eyes pop open as the sensation of being engulfed in his mouth overwhelms me.

He's clearly done this before. He does things to me I can't describe. He uses his tongue in ways that I have no names for. I cry out, unable to stop myself as I wither under him, but he keeps me anchored to the blanket with his strong hands and arms.

I feel myself nearing the edge. But this time it is different from when I am alone. It's long, drawn out, and more intense. Alone sessions usually consist of me rubbing myself to orgasm for the sake of relieving pressure. This is something else.

It's like he's drawing it out of me and it isn't just centered at the length of me. I feel like every part of me is on fire. Every nerve ending is reacting. My skin is hot and flushed and my fingers and toes clench as my muscles freeze and release. He uses his mouth to draw it out and I hear the broken cries and pleas as I shout his name. He focuses his attention of the sensitive underside of me and that's when he pushes me over the edge. I cling to him as he works me over and I feel like he has split my body into a million pieces. I shiver under him in the aftermath as he flexes and shifts, trying to adjust himself so he is more comfortable.

I gaze up at him through a hazy, cloudy vision. There are

spots in front of my eyes that I continue to try to blink away. After a few moments, my breathing calms and I manage to croak out, "If you want...we could...you haven't." He kisses my babbling away, guessing at what I am offering him.

"Yes, God yes I want that. But it won't be tonight," he tells me. Consciousness fully returns, and I sit up on one elbow.

"Why not? Is it something I did?" I ask tentatively.

"No," he explains as he rubs the back of my neck. Orgasms have made my neck tense before, but never to this extent. He must sense this, or experienced it himself, because he has been rubbing the tension away ever since he lay back down beside me. "That is going to be fun, and pleasurable, we're both going to pass out from it after because I intend to make it everything you fantasize about, but it is going to leave you a little sore the next day," he confesses. It doesn't worry me. I don't think he is going to intentionally hurt me. It's just the reality of the act. I get why he is holding off though. "We both need to dance tomorrow and to the absolute best of our abilities."

I can't leave him in this state though. Pleasing me had pushed him to the edge of his breaking point, just as it had done to me.

I shimmy back down the blanket and his thighs tremble as I place my palms on either one and push them back so that I can get at him.

"Please, don't tease." His voice is low and guttural. His eyes are wide and wild, and I nod my head before I lower my mouth back on him, giving him exactly the kind of attention he needs. It doesn't take him long. Soon I have my first experience moving a man to orgasm and I revel in the feel of him rocking back and forth underneath me. I react on instinct, which seems to be the right thing to do, as he had done for me, and then I crawl back up the length of him and collapse in his arms as we both doze off for a time, wrapped up in each other.

When the cold gets to be too much, we begrudgingly pull ourselves up and make our way back downstairs to the dorms to sleep for the remainder of the night. He doesn't even bother returning to his dorm, he crawls into bed beside me, pulling me to him and falling fast asleep within the span of minutes. I drift off just as content, lying next to him and wake to the sound of the alarm, announcing the day of tryouts.

CHAPTER NINE

*A*fter a hurried shower and breakfast, we make our way to the auditorium, where Madame Roussou and Mr. Schlewp sit behind a desk with papers in front of them. There is another impartial judge from the music department, as he will be conducting the band from the pit for the music pieces.

We catch up with Katarina and the rest of the drama club who are re-reading lines, and stretching to the best of their ability for the dance routines they had picked out. I join her and a small group of her friends, as Gregor makes his way around the group saying good morning to everyone. I notice how they all look between us and smile, and I wonder if it's that obvious, what we had done on the rooftop the night before. The memory fills me with euphoria, just the boost I need to set myself into the mindset to perform as best as I can.

I stretch as I read lines and I jump up and down, keeping myself warmed up, as one-by-one the students and their partners are called to the stage. Katarina leaves us about an hour later, and I pause long enough to watch her audition, which isn't too bad. She had elected to audition by herself rather than with a partner, as she had explained at breakfast. She didn't want to drag anyone down if she was already mud in the eyes of Madame. I tried to assure her that that wasn't the case, and she just shrugged and laughed it off.

As the time grew nearer and nearer for Gregor and I to perform, the lead in my stomach turned to flighty butterflies, and I had a hard time keeping that morning's breakfast down. We made our way behind stage to wait for our names to be called, and with only one audition in front of us, my nerves began to get the better of me. I didn't know how Gregor could stand there, calm and collected, but the third time I paced by him, he grabbed my arm and spun me into him.

No one could see us in the shadow of the curtains. Or at least, that is what I was telling myself and trying to convince myself to believe. Gregor pulled me into a gentle kiss which instantly calmed me somehow. His puffy lips grazing over mine were a soothing balm to my nerves. It's as if he was saying, "I've got you" with a kiss.

"Calm down," he whispered in my ear. "Remember the dance and let yourself feel it, OK?" he asked. I nodded as our names were called and he released me.

As we moved on stage, he pointed between us and I nodded again as I focused on him and him alone. The music started, a piece we had chosen together, and as I moved toward him, the rest of the world fell away. We moved together as a cohesive unit, allowing the music and the dance to wash over us as we told a story of the war of wills and the battle of outside discrimination. There wasn't one misstep or wrong turn, and as we finished the dance, the entire auditorium was silent for a few moments, before everyone burst into cheers and clapping.

Even Madame Roussou gave me a nod of approval as she made some markings on her clipboard.

After a bow, Gregor gave my hand a squeeze and left the stage for me to perform the classical piece. I performed it again, flawlessly, as I was drunk on the euphoria of the last performance. When I was done, I moved stage left and he performed his piece, only stumbling in a few places, but for a drama student, he did remarkably well with the choreography. We then did the reading together, and I only had to whisper, "Line" once to pick up a line I had forgotten.

As we exited the stage, I launched myself at him and we hugged each other in triumph for such an amazing audition, and then in turn gave hugs to Katarina and his friends who were waiting for us backstage. I couldn't have felt better about an audition than I had in my entire dancing career, and it was made all the sweeter by Gregor's presence.

The next week was a nightmare waiting for the results to post, and my euphoria came crashing down around me when I read the casting post a week later. I had been cast as the understudy to Eric. I stood, staring at the notice board, realizing that even with the hard work and the excellent audition, there were some things in this world that were just handed to others because of their looks or the way their body was built.

I pushed through the crowd and ran up the stairs, all the way to the roof access before I realized, I didn't have a key. I kept fighting back the burn in my eyes as I tried to turn around and flee the landing, to go back to my room where I could have a moment of privacy. But when I turned back around, strong arms encircled me, and for the first time since I had admitted to myself, or anyone else that I was gay and I wanted to be a dancer, I cried about the pain, hurt, and humiliation of discrimination that I had received because of it.

I vaguely remember Gregor unlocking the door and pulling us onto the rooftop, where we sank to the ground and he held me and rocked me. He didn't comment on my tears. He let me suffer in peace and misery as I wept. He would never tell anyone about them either, for which I was grateful. He understood and even if he isn't the kind of guy to cry, he let me know it was ok.

When my eyes dried up and my hiccups stopped, I sat back and patted at the wet spot on his t-shirt, feeling the flood of embarrassment run through me and hit my cheeks.

"Sorry," I whispered through a raw choked voice.

"There's nothing to be sorry for," he told me firmly, cupping my chin and forcing me to look at him. "It's bullshit that men think they can't cry," he tells me. "It's also bullshit that Eric got that part, and we both know it."

I nod, not really wanting to think about the musical anymore. It isn't like my dancing career is over. I have two more years to go, and I'll still be a member of the core dancers. I suddenly feel ashamed that I hadn't looked to see if Gregor had been cast.

"Did you get it? I'm sorry, I didn't…" I trail off. He gives me a squeeze of reassurance.

"It's ok. I did get the role of Tom Collins. It looks like no one got the role they expected, but everyone who was auditioning for a lead, got a lead…except…" He hugs me tighter, not wanting to have caused me any more pain.

"Except me," I mumble into his chest. "I suppose this means you are going to be insanely busy now. And I won't see you as much up here," I comment, miserably.

"Yeah, maybe. You still need to understudy for the part of Angel for Eric though," he mentions. My stomach feels sick as I remember the satisfied look on Eric's face as I pushed my way through the crowd. He had gotten a lead again, and I didn't. He had also gotten the lead of the love interest to Gregor's character, and I didn't. He knew that working so closely with Gregor was going to eat away at me. As if sensing my apprehension to this, Gregor continues. "It changes nothing for us," he tells me.

I sit back and gaze up at him as he stares down at me. "I mean it, Colin. It changes nothing about the way I feel about you, so don't you for one second think that you don't mean the world to me," he finishes. "Understand?" he asks.

I nod my head and settle back down in his lap. All too soon, his phone beeps, indicating that we need to get to class and begin rehearsals. I stand up, brushing the gravel from my tights, and rubbing anxiously at my eyes which feel swollen and puffy. Gregor grips my wrists and moves my hands away.

"It's going to be alright," he says. "You're going to walk with me downstairs to rehearsal, look them all in the face with your head up, with me right by your side, holding your hand." I nod and link my fingers with his. It's a sight the rest of the students have become accustomed to over the last two weeks, and I know somehow, I am going to make it through this with him.

When we get to the studio, a congregation of students has amassed in the hallway as we wait for Madame to let us in. When she unlocks the door to the studio, I march straight past her and don't say a word, not looking her in the face as she tries to catch my eye. We both know my audition was flawless, and her ideals for classism had skewed her judging scores. Eric's choreographed piece had just been another rendition of a classical piece, and hadn't provided any new introspect to the dancing at all.

The first class is almost unbearable as I feel people stare at Gregor and I and whisper. I suppose it comes with the hazard of dating, but I can't help but silently loathe them and their gossiping as I somehow, miraculously make it through the first session. What comes as the hardest part is when I am sitting in my dorm that evening, and Katarina comes in with tissues, ice cream, and movies when it is time for Gregor to get up and have his first solo session with Eric. It's unbearable watching him go, even though I know as an understudy I will have to join him tomorrow to begin watching Eric as he works through the moves.

Madame had indicated she wanted the leads to have one-on-one time with her the first night, so she could get a feeling for the dynamic of the group. Several drama students, Gregor, Eric, and Angela were amongst those students. Katarina had been cast only as an understudy as well.

The first couple of weeks feel like pure torture as I watch Eric get closer and closer to Gregor. Sometimes their heads are bent low as they work through lines together, or they are within inches of each other's faces. The love scene is set to be rehearsed next week, and it makes me sick to my stomach to think about the two of them interacting that way. Gregor spends most nights with me, crawling into bed late at night after a particularly grueling session. Madame often keeps him and the other leads late to have chats with them as she likes to call it. Mostly they are talks which nitpick their performances and she tells them ways they can improve. I toss and turn most nights, unable to sleep.

The week of the love scene comes into swing and that afternoon, when the drama students join us, I stare blankly at the barre where I am stretching as I listen to Eric offer Gregor advice on how they can make it have a full erotic effect for the audience.

Katarina catches my eye in the mirror and offers me a sympathetic look, and I realize the only solution I have to this problem was the right one all along. Gregor, without meaning to, has become a distraction and a detriment to my dancing. I work through the conversation in my head about the break up I am planning that evening in our usual five minutes of free time get away on the roof. That is until I hear a sharp scream of pain, and I look over and see Eric, writhing on the floor in agony, clutching his ankle.

CHAPTER TEN

"They say it was sprained, if not fractured," Gregor tells me at dinner that night.

"Huh?" I ask. The hours that had passed as the ambulance came and I had stepped in as the understudy, seemed to pass by in a haze. Madame had accompanied Eric to the hospital, and Mr. Schlewp had taken over the session, but not allowed us to dance under the dire warning from Madame.

"I overheard Angela talking with Madame Roussou. Apparently, he hasn't been practicing or stretching to accommodate freestyle dancing, and only continuing to do ballet exercises. He didn't think it was necessary for them because dancing is all he does anyway. Freestyle, combined with the ballet moves, is a completely different way of dancing, using completely different muscles sometimes. He didn't account for the fact that he would be in a nontraditional costume, and interacting with props. He tripped over one of the props on the floor that was being used. He went down, and the rest is history," Gregor explained.

I had just gotten done from a grueling session with Madame, who demanded I stay over the Christmas break for extra sessions to catch me up to speed with the rest of the leads. I was tired and ached all over, and she was going with Eric tomorrow for more x-rays, which would give me one blissful morning of peace and quiet as she accompanied him to the hospital. He had come back in a cast and the entire company fawned over him, as Madame cornered me and immediately began to work on my subpar form.

When that session had gotten over, I was still in a daze as I made my way to the dining hall. On the one hand, the stress of not having to worry about Gregor and Eric becoming too close was gone. But on the other, my malcontent had grown exponentially over the last couple of weeks. Internally I was berating myself, thinking I was a terrible person for secretly being relieved. An injury like that could potentially cost Eric his entire career if he doesn't follow exact doctor's orders. As much as I dislike the guy and don't like him close to my boyfriend, I would never wish an injury like that on another dancer.

I barely touch my dinner as I listen to Gregor and the others recount what had happened. After a few moments, Angela begins to cry into her salad, having been terribly affected by the loss of her lead in Swan Lake. Gregor turns to me as others dole sympathy on her, with the exception of Katarina and I, because this could potentially be the break I need in my own career.

"Do you want to go upstairs and get away?" Gregor asks softly.

"Yeah, I think that's a good idea," I murmur. We quietly excuse ourselves as Angela continues to sob. The drama department is hanging on her every word as we retreat out the door. I vaguely feel bad for them that they have been sucked up into her drama, but then she'll fit with them nicely at the end of the musical. She had been cast as Mimi, the lead female who comes with her own set of drama and issues, so Angela will have no problem fitting the role well.

I trudge up the stairs heavily. Tonight it feels like I'm marching towards a prison sentence than a place of respite.

When we get out onto the roof, Gregor turns to me and says, "I won't let you break up with me. Not over this. His accident was not your fault," he says quietly.

I blink at him, and then I feel anger rage through me. "Not my fault? How is it not my fault? I practically willed the guy dead and then this happens. I loathed you for being so close to him when I couldn't touch you! You never noticed me standing there watching you when those moments came, and it felt like I was dying inside when you didn't see me. So, tell me again, how this is not my fault."

"You didn't put that prop there. And you didn't cause Eric to neglect his duty and diligence as a performer to himself and the company. His arrogance caused his accident. Ballet isn't the only form of expression. Now, as for ignoring you, we both figured this issue would come up at some point, and we agreed to work through it when the time came. Well, here it is. I told you it changes nothing between us, and I meant it. I won't let you throw away what we have, because I still honestly believe we are better for having it," he finishes.

I pace the rooftop, angry and confused. It would be so much easier if I just broke things off with him and focused, like I originally intended, on the dance. It would be easier, in theory, but having to work with him daily now? Being that close, there is no way I wouldn't want to be back in his arms again. I don't know what to say, so I continue to stomp around the rooftop as he watches me.

A couple of times I pause and look at him, ready to say something, anything, but the words get stuck. Finally, I blurt out, "you can't force me to be in a relationship with you."

I feel stupid the minute I say it. Anger flares in his eyes and I wonder at what his breaking point is. I know I'm new to the gay relationship ventures, but at some point, his endless amount of patience is going to run out with me. However, he takes a deep breath and releases it, indicating that it is not going to be tonight.

"You're right. I can't force you to be in a relationship with me. I can however, point out that we have something between us. Something neither one of us can deny. If you need some space while you get your head in the game, if you want me to back off a little while you get accustomed to the schedule, I can back down. But I am not going anywhere. Remember that. When you're ready, you come and find me because I'm right here."

With that, he turns and walks back to the door to leave me with my thoughts. He props it open so that I'm not locked outside, and I take a few steps toward him as he turns his back and leaves. I'm not sure what I would say to him. "Stay. Don't go. I'm an idiot and don't know what I'm doing." All seem like perfectly plausible things to say, but when I open my mouth to say them, the words get stuck somewhere between my brain and my emotionally confused heart. I kick gravel at the door in frustration and turn away.

The tracks from where we have danced together are all over the roof. Some of the paths are beginning to fade under the elements, but most of them are in wide swooping circles. I walk some of the arcs in an attempt to clear my head. I consider putting some music on from my phone and dancing my stress away, but I realize for the first time in as long as I can remember, my reason for dancing, the desire and passion I have for it, is gone. It just walked through that door and walked away from me in the form of Gregor. To chase after him now would be desperate. He's not wrong, I need to work through some of my emotions before I go to him again.

I sink to my knees and rock back and forth for a long time as I try to sort them out inside. But the more I try, the more jumbled they get. I continue to rock myself when the rain starts. It beats down on me in hard pelting, torrential downpours, and it feels like my soul is weeping right along with it. This is where I remain for a long while. It's also where Katarina comes to find me, apparently hours later, when I didn't turn up for our scheduled movie night. It was meant to help us relax for an hour or two before going to bed, because the next day would be just as hard and difficult. Katarina sits in the rain with me and when I next look up, tears are streaming down her face too.

"What is it? What's wrong?" I ask.

"I told my parents I am switching programs."

My stomach sinks. I can sense her world crashing down around her, just like mine has. "What happened?" I ask hesitantly.

"They told me they wouldn't pay for me to attend Julliard if I do. I spoke with administration and I would have to do the work study program if I want to stay."

The work study program isn't bad, and she knows this. It's the fight with her parents that has her completely wrecked like I am. I pull her into my arms, and we sit in the rain, drenched through to the bone on the rooftop, and we cry for ourselves and each other as we work through our misery. The only glimmer of hope remaining in us is that we have each other as best friends to get through all this. It's what motivates us to get up out of the puddle of water, and return to the dorms to get dried and get some sleep. Somehow, we know we will find the will and the way to continue on the next day. We fall asleep next to one another as we watch the dancing hippos in Fantasia.

CHAPTER ELEVEN

*T*he next day I wake, and my arm is numb. I realize there is no feeling in it, because Katarina is lying next to me and using the crook of it as a pillow. I lie there, staring at the boring beige ceiling, wondering how on earth I am going to make it through the next few weeks of rehearsal with Gregor in such close proximity. It's going to be torturous, to be that close but not truly have him. He's given me the choice to come and find him, of course. But what does that really mean? Does he want me to divide my attention between him and dancing? He said that wasn't it, but how do I choose a man who has given me an ultimatum I don't understand?

I sigh and turn my head to the night stand.

"Oh no! Ohhhh no!" I sit up hastily, jostling Katarina awake.

"Hey!," she glares at me.

"We're late! We're late for rehearsal!," I panic. I rip my tights while pulling it on in a rush. "Damn it!" I snap as I grab my bag. "Come on Katarina, we're late. Get up!" I shout at her.

"You might be late, but drama classes don't start for another two hours." She grumbles and rolls back over in my bed.

I had completely forgotten that the drama program starts at seven in the morning, not five. I grab my bag and dash out the door and down the navy blue and white colored hallways. I skid to a halt outside the studio door and peer inside. The entire company is halfway through warm ups as I push my way inside and grab the empty slot on the closest end of the barre.

"How good of you to join us." Madame's voice cuts through the soft swooshing of limbs from across the studio. I plie and move my right foot up into second position from first before bowing and moving to third.

"I'm sorry Madame," I murmur. Her withering stare cuts through me as I bring my foot back into fourth position.

I half expected her to continue berating me in front of the entire class. It's bad enough Eric is sitting in his cast in a metal folding chair in the center of the mirror watching all of us and smirking. When I hear the clunk of Madame's cane on the floor as it approaches, I cringe in anticipation of what is to come.

She surprises me though. I feel her withered hand wrap around my arm and tug me away from the barre and toward the door. Is she kicking me out? I look desperately around the rest of the class whose faces remain mostly passive as I allow myself to be steered into the hallway. Angela and Eric are the only ones with the satisfied smug look on their faces, and a few of the other classmates almost look at me pityingly.

The door shuts softly behind us and I look back through the window one more time before I follow Madame as she stumps her way down the hall. She doesn't say a word as she walks, and I dutifully follow her, all the way through the school and into the auditorium.

When we get there, she climbs the stairs on the side of the stage and I walk behind her as she walks around the stage and looks out over the rows and rows of red velvet seats that sit empty, but sit, looking back at us like blank faces, waiting for the performance to begin.

"Do you know why I picked you to come to Julliard?" she asks suddenly. I stop beside her as we stand center stage and look out over the rows of empty seats.

"Because of my performance in Lord of the Dance," I answer promptly. My performance had been flawless.

"No. I may have been in attendance at that performance, but that isn't why I even deemed you worthy enough to speak to after that dance."

"I'm confused then, Madame."

"I picked you because you tried. You, the little Irish boy from Boston, got up on that stage despite the fact that you have that God awful red hair and the fact that you're an inch shorter than the typical six-foot Danseur."

"I still don't understand, Madame. Of course, I tried. I rehearsed for that performance for months."

"Ah, yes. You still don't understand what I mean. Any dancer is going to practice until the moves are flawless. That is the expectation. So is getting to rehearsals on time, and wearing the appropriate, neat and tidy apparel, I might add." She gives my tights a shrewd look and I cross my leg behind the other, rubbing the back of my foot in a pretend motion to hide the rip. She continues, ignoring the motion. "Eric is always going to have an advantage over you. He will always be better technically because he has the dancer's body type. His presence with his dark hair and his dark eyes, stands out in a way that won't for you. If anyone notices you, it will be because of your differences, but that isn't necessarily a good thing."

If Madame is trying to make me feel better about anything, she sure does have a round about way of doing it, but then she has often proven to march to the beat of her own drum.

"Eric always has been and always will be, the best."

"OK," I'm still not sure where this is going.

"The reason Eric will never see more than ten years as a dancer, however, is because he doesn't try." I raise my eyebrows at her, jaw dropping. "Sure, he can perform the moves, but he doesn't need to try to work hard at them, because he has always been cast into the favorable light, making it easier for him by far. You, on the other hand, will always have to work hard. You'll always have to make sacrifices and you'll always prove to people time and time again that where you belong is on the dance floor, because whether it is professionally or personally, that is where people are always going to find you. It's where your Gregor found you that night after the announcement of the musical, but don't make the mistake for one minute in thinking he was the only one watching you."

"Madame-"

She waves her hand, cutting me off. "I realize students think when I ask for sacrifices it means I'm asking them to cut out their personal lives, but in fact, it doesn't. I'm asking students to sacrifice the typical college behavior. The drinking and the parties and the late nights. That does not include their reason for dancing. What makes them passionate that they are so overwhelmed with emotion, that they must express it with the use of their bodies. That day on the stage in Boston, you had something to say. You were telling the whole world you were the Irish underdog, but you were going to dance until there were scorch marks on the floor and smoke on your heels just to show everyone. I admired that. How hard you tried. That is why I chose you for Julliard."

"And how does this all pertain to me being late for class this morning Madame?" I ask softly. I had never thought she had seen anything special in me, rather it was the recruiter who found, whatever it was that they were looking for and pushed her to it. In the year and a half that I have known Madame, I should have realized she isn't the kind of woman to be pushed to anything she doesn't want to do.

"Not a damn thing."

I stifle a laugh. Usually when she swears at us, it is in rapid French. We've all come to pick up some of her sayings and understand on a level of how screwed we are from, *"Mon Dieu, aide-moi s'il te plaît"* to *"Bon sang! Comment puis-je enseigner les babouins avec les pieds de plomb?"*

"I'm telling you all this," she explains, "because you have a chance here, not just with Swan Lake, but with this musical. To show everyone how hard you try. At the end of a dancer's career, they need to look back on it and without a shadow of a doubt, say to themselves that they danced until they simply couldn't dance anymore."

"Yes, Madame."

"I don't know what is going on with you, Eric, and that Gregor kid. What I do know is when you started choreographing your piece for the audition and I watched you dance here on the stage in an empty auditorium, you had something else to say. Whatever that was, you need to find it again, Colin. Because that's the kind of dancing I want to see when you perform on Valentine's Day," she finishes.

Madame had never indicated whether she approved or disapproved of relationships. I always had the preconceptions that she wanted dancers to focus on their career. It appears as if she is saying she wants her dancers to embrace whatever makes them passionate about the dance. I stare at her a long moment before I ask,

"Why did you bring me here this morning?"

"Because, we need to get you up to speed. Eric can run the class in my absence. But as understudy, you know all the moves. You've rehearsed, and you've worked until you could perform the steps in your sleep. Now you need to try to dance."

She walks over to a chair on the side of the stage and sits down. I stare at her a moment, wondering what she wants me to do, and then I look out into the auditorium, feeling stupid that I'm going to dance for an old woman, without music or an audience, and somehow feel like I am connecting with the passion for dancing. I look back at her one more time and she nods, resigned not to say another word until I show her what I have been repressing for weeks now. I briefly wonder why she chose me as understudy, if she felt like I have something more than Eric, but then she had already answered that question for me too. She's grooming Eric. Grooming him to be the exceptional dancer, for the next ten years, and then he will move on to something like teaching and coaching, just like her. I smile at the knowledge that she has faith in my passion that I will continue even after the optimum age and let that burning light inside me shine through.

I close my eyes and begin to move, swaying side to side, searching for the internal rhythm that has almost been extinguished. I find it, deep down as I sashay to the right, avoiding a puddle on the rooftop. I pirouette, letting the rain drops spray from my limbs as I move across the roof. I open my eyes, faltering a little as I arabesque on the stage and catch sight of Madame, but I quickly bow deeper into the move, bending low before the image of my Dad, almost as if begging for his acceptance. I rise and take a running leap, as I grand jeté towards the fantasy of Gregor on the opposite side of the stage standing there with open arms. I soubresaut with Katarina, jumping up and down swiftly and suddenly as we celebrate in excitement her decision to change majors, something we should have done to begin with last night on the rooftop, instead of becoming depressed and melancholy because of the actions and judgments of others.

As I perform a Temps levé, I kick out my worries, stress and fear, from side to side, foot to foot. I cast it away in the action and free myself to find the inner music. I focus on the rhythm as the names of the moves slip away and my body takes over, performing the actions out of muscle memory rather than concentration. I find the music to dance to in my soul. I'd been hearing it all my life, even before the dancing with Gregor on the rooftop.

"Honk! Beep! Beep! Screech! Hey! - Honk! Beep! Beep! Thwack! How are you?- Honk! Beep! Beep! Smack! Taxi!"

The music of my life begins to take over and I move, forgetting that I am in the auditorium, that I am at Julliard, that I have worried and stressed about perfection since having arrived there. I'd been dancing to this tune my entire life, trading one city for another, and in this city, finding Gregor to only add to the rhythm.

"Honk! Beep! Beep! Hi, I'm Gregor. – Honk! Beep! Beep! Click! I'm Colin. – Honk! Beep! Beep! Dance with me Colin."

I twirl endlessly around the stage, imagining I am back in Gregor's arms and allowing myself to be led through this dance, through life with him there as my dance partner through it all. I realize, with alacrity, as I finally come to a sweeping bow down from a flying pas de chat, that it's what I was missing all along.

I'm sweating and red faced as I look over and see Madame rocking back and forth in the chair smiling.

"Good, very good. Whatever that was, whoever you just danced with or for, I want you to keep that in mind every day for the next few weeks until the show. Understood?"

I nod and say nothing. I don't need to explain what it was to her. Some things are private, and she understands this. I walk back with her to class in silence and by then the class is warmed up and paired off. Angela had been dancing alone until I re-enter with Madame, and I pair up with her.

She stiffens in my arms and it makes for an interesting rehearsal, trying to stay on form. I know she prefers to dance with Eric, and he is constantly gimping over to us on his crutches to criticize my form, when in fact I know she is the one that needs to loosen up. But this time, their snide remarks and smug expressions don't register in my mind at all. I focus on the classical music that is playing as we rehearse the steps of Swan Lake, but the fire in my heart for the dance, and for my feelings which I had been denying about Gregor all this time, drown out any negativity that is thrown my way through rehearsal.

I know it will take a lot to make amends with Gregor, and we still have to work through the performance and the practices for the Valentine's Day Virtuoso, but I am confident that somehow, I can make it all work out.

I'm feeling really confident about all of this, until the drama students enter for the mid-morning practice and Katarina walks in side by side with Gregor, but he refuses to look at me.

CHAPTER TWELVE

"*L*et's take it from the top!" Mr. Schlewp calls. He pushes his glasses up on his face and glances down at his script. He had been writing and scribbling notes on it with every re-run. I had barely caught Gregor's eye except when it was called for in the script.

Today we were working strictly on lines and acting, and not the choreographed musical pieces, so although there was interaction with one another, not nearly so much as the physical contact that was called for during the performance numbers.

I glanced in a panic back at Katarina. She looks strange in her street clothes with the rest of the drama students. They all have on sweatpants and t-shirts, where the dancers have their unitards and tights. She looks between me and Gregor and shrugs. I wince when I see him shove Seth playfully, wondering if maybe I really blew it big time last night.

As we take our places again, Gregor turns his head and the light of the weak sunshine outside catches his eyes and they seem to shine, but I notice the twinkle in his eye is cast over his shoulder at Seth who had just been goofing around with him. When he turns back to me, his expression isn't angry, it's worse. He pastes a completely placid look on his face and I can't get a read on his emotions at all.

I offer him a weak smile and for a moment he looks like he is going to say something, but then Mr. Schlewp calls, "Action!"

The words for the characters come out automatically, but they feel like they are lacking in sincerity to me. Maybe I'm just reading too much into it. I'm not sure, but they definitely feel forced.

When class breaks for lunch, I jog over to Katarina and ask, "Did he say anything before you guys came into class?" We stand watching him as he tousles the hair of Katie, a bohemian style actress with ginger hair and freckles that splatter her cheeks and face. I become transfixed in his laugh, having missed it even though only a night has passed.

"Yeah, he welcomed me to the drama program and told me it was about time."

My stomach drops. I was hoping if he spoke to anyone about last night, it would have been Katarina. I give her a quick, half-hearted smile. "Hey, I should have said congrats too! I'm sorry I was such a downer last night. You've got enough to think about, I should have been a better friend and been happy for you." I give her a hug as we walk out the classroom door.

"It's ok, Colin. You had your mind on other things, I can completely understand that." She links her arm with mine and pats the back of my hand reassuringly.

"Can we just skip the dining hall today?" I ask her. She pauses as she looks after the drama crowd and I quickly say, "never mind. I know you want to hang out and fit in with the new crowd. That was selfish of me to ask."

"Honestly, Colin, you need to learn that you're my BFF here. If you need a break from the scene, of course I'll come hang out with you. If you turn into a social recluse however, then we're going to have an intervention."

We turn and start walking back down the hall toward the dorms. Katarina keeps a stash of food in her dorm and she hands me a bag of chips as she shoves a couple of Hot Pockets in the microwave and nukes them, so they are soggy on the inside and chewy on the outer crust. They aren't the most appetizing of lunches, but I'm grateful for the peace and quiet.

She flips on the t.v. and we sit on the bed gnawing at the cardboard-like pizza crusts and the midday news comes on.

I watch as the lanky newscaster in his well-fitted suit comes on. He's standing at a dockside and there are workers scurrying behind him as he begins speaking.

"In a tragic accident that left one longshoreman dead and five others injured, an explosion rocked the docks here in South Boston last night. However, it is known that four of the injured are related. Not a lot is known about the cause of the explosion, it is suspected that it might have to do with the rivalries between the Irish mob families, O'Duffy and O'Callaghan. There has been a long-standing feud between the two families that has been the cause of several homicides and suspected fights that have broken out. This particular shipping yard, O'Duffy's Importing and Exporting, is owned and operated by James O'Duffy, suspected leader of the O'Duffy mob family. The workers are not being very forthcoming with information regarding the explosion and all O'Duffy had to say was he hopes those injured in the blast have a speedy recovery and that he is working closely with the family affected by the tragic accident."

My body freezes as I watch in horror as the cameraman zooms in on the shipping container that has a hole in it the size of a wrecking ball. I would have suspected that was the cause, except for the noticeable scorch marks around the hole, and the obvious signs of debris littering the docks. My mouth goes dry and I set the plate of the Hot Pockets down beside me as I lean forward toward the television screen.

"Show me, show us who was hurt," I urge the telecaster.

"Colin, isn't that…don't your Dad and brothers work at O'Duffy's?" Katarina asks in a horrified whisper.

"Show me, show us who was hurt." I can feel my body rocking back and forth on the bed, although my mind feels detached as it remains concentrated on the screen. Surely someone would have called me if the four were…but, it's such a large dock and a lot of families have multiple fathers and sons working down there. There's thousands of workers, it can't be…

My blood runs cold as the footage changes from the shipping container back to the broadcaster, who begins to rattle off the names of the injured. "Due to privacy, the family of the deceased is requesting their loved one be kept out of the news, but the four who were injured and sent to Our Lady of the Peace Medical Hospital, a well-known private Catholic Hospital are head of household Finn O'Shea and his three sons Patrick, Liam, and Seamus. It is known to us that there is a fourth son, but he has been unable to be reached for comment and if he will pick up work at O'Duffy's to continue supporting his family."

"Turn it off," I whisper. Katarina immediately jumps off the bed and switches the t.v. off. I stand, pacing the tiny room and kicking aside an assortment of clothes, books and dirty dishes. Her room is decorated in all her favorite movie posters. The colors shine back at me on glossy paper that is chaotic, and the swirl of colors makes me dizzy.

I stop near the doorway, thinking I should call Mum, but then, she would be at the hospital.

"Colin?" Katarina says tentatively, like I might break at the slightest touch or sound. I look at her and wipe the sweat from my hands on my tights and then keel over, grabbing her trash can near the door.

By the time I'm done being sick and emptying the contents of the pizza pockets from my stomach, I am shaking all over and my stomach muscles ache.

"Colin, you're in shock." She rubs my back and places a blanket over my shoulders as I begin to shiver. "I've sent for help." She tells me, and I nod numbly.

A moment later I hear the tell-tale signs of Madame thunking down the hall as fast as she can with her cane. Katarina goes to the door and waves her inside.

"He's here. He's in here," she proclaims.

Madame pushes her way into the room, followed closely by Mr. Schlewp and to my surprise, Gregor.

"We've just heard. Of course, you are being dismissed early for the Christmas holidays..." Mr. Schlewp babbles. Madame sits at Katarina's desk chair staring at my pale sweaty face.

"Do you need us to give you an extended leave of absence?" she asks quietly. I frown at her, not sure what she is asking so I shake my head.

"N...no Madame. I just need to get to the hospital." I tell her. She stares at me for a long moment and then shakes her head.

"I can take him," Katarina says quietly. Mr. Schlewp and Madame agree and then Gregor speaks up.

"I'll go with them. I'm from South Boston, that part of the city...it's best if you travel in a group.

"Are you sure that's a good idea?" Mr. Schlewp asks. "The show is only a couple of months away. We really could practice..."

"I'm going," Gregor states firmly. "If the school needs to punish me or, I don't know, kick me out. Well then, that's that."

Mr. Schlewp and Madame look at each other and then Madame says, "Very well. The school is not going to kick you out and you will not be punished for leaving. We need you back as the lead in your part. You may take your Christmas holiday early too, but we'll need you back here before New Year's for rehearsals. We'll have a lot of time to make up for. Colin, if you can't come back, we completely understand, so just send word as soon as you can. We understand you have more pressing concerns right now than the show."

I nod at them again, feeling like at any moment my brain will kick on and this feeling of stupidity and cloudiness will leave my vision. Mr. Schlewp and Madame stand, each patting me on the shoulder and offering their condolences before they leave. Katarina jumps up in a whirlwind of activity as she throws some clothes and toiletries in a bag. Gregor sits on the bed beside me and his big body radiates heat that I find comforting. I sway towards him, but catch myself from leaning on him just in time before my shoulder makes contact.

As if sensing my need to make contact, he slips his fingers through mine, interlocking them and squeezing my palm. The contact is reassuring, and I sigh, slouching my shoulders, feeling suddenly exhausted to my very core. When Katarina is done, she glances between us but says nothing about the hand holding.

"Come on Colin, let's go to your room and pack some things for vacation and then Gregor can go to his room and pack his bag."

I nod numbly and stand, swaying again. My stomach feels weak and the nausea rolls through me in a wave.

"I think your hot pockets were bad," I blurt.

Katarina opens her mouth to say something, shuts it when she thinks better of it, then says, "yeah, OK. Thanks."

We walk down the halls and other students stare at me as I pass by. Word has spread rapidly about the explosion and whose family was affected.

"You don't have to do this," I turn to Gregor and say.

He looks at me with his solemn dark eyes and says, "I'm coming with you and that's non-negotiable. Now pack your bag. I'll be back in ten minutes."

He pulls me into a hug and I lose myself in his intoxicating scent. His hug seems to glue the pieces back together of my shattered reality and I know that somehow in the next ten minutes, I am going to make it through. I enter my dorm and pull out a few pairs of jeans and sweatpants and t-shirts. It takes me half the time to pack my bag than Katarina because my room is so neat and orderly. I find it funny that even with her dorm in complete disarray and having to work through the fight with her parents, of the two of us, my life has somehow become more chaotic. Or maybe I am just being selfish in my internal pity party. Maybe it's not fair to play the "my pain is worse than your pain" game in my head.

Whatever Katarina may be feeling, she graciously doesn't let on as she sits on my bed and watches me move around the room woodenly.

When Gregor returns a few minutes later with his duffel bag thrown over his shoulder, he picks up Katarina's and we all head outside and hail a cab to the train station.

The trip is a silent one. Katarina sits opposite of Gregor and I, and I claim the window seat, staring absentmindedly out and not really seeing the buildings and houses go by. They soon give way to more rural residences and the occasional areas where we pass through towns, but it all bleeds together in my mind.

Are they going to be alright? How badly were they injured? Will they be able to go back to work? I don't know how to be a long-shoreman. If Mum needs a man to be the breadwinner of the house, I never learned a skill or trade. I've always been a dancer. How will she afford the cost of the medical bills? Will O'Duffy give her compensation?

My mind races with thoughts as fast as the moving train. It seems like the ride takes all day when in fact, it only takes a few hours. Katarina goes to the dining cart and buys some sandwiches for lunch, but the slightly wilted lettuce on mine has my stomach turning over again. If she's offended that I didn't eat the sandwich, she doesn't say so. Gregor offers me his water and I gladly take a few refreshing sips of that. It doesn't make my stomach churn like the thought of food does, so he waves his hand at it when I try to hand it back to him.

I gratefully press it between my knees as I turn back to the window, occasionally picking it up to take sips.

We roll into South Station and I jump up, cracking my forehead on the overhead luggage rack.

"Damn it!" I hiss, rubbing the spot gingerly. I can already tell it's going to leave a bruise and a headache in its wake. But no amount of pain compares to the anxiety of losing my Dad and my brothers.

When we disembark and step out onto the platform, I look around for an available taxi and sense Katarina and Gregor right at my heels. As we have come in during the evening rush hour, there aren't any taxis available, so I set off down the street in the direction of the hospital. It's a fair distance from the station, but I am determined to make it to the hospital, even if it means having to walk.

"Hey, hold up Colin," Gregor's voice sounds in my ear. "We can't walk through South Boston, especially this time of night. And if you head in the direction you are, that way lies trouble, even if it's a short cut," he reasons.

"I don't care Gregor. It's my family!" I shout at him, finally losing my composure. He holds his hands up and steps back.

"All I'm saying is, I texted my Mom and she's on her way over with the van and she's willing to drive us there," He murmurs.

Several bystanders stare at us and I glower at them, so they lower their eyes and move away quickly.

"I think waiting the few minutes for Ms. McCallum is a good idea, Colin," Katarina pleads. "I don't know this city, but I trust that you and Gregor do. We will get to the hospital, I promise."

Her face is white and pinched, and my bluster blows out. They are here for me and just trying to help.

"I'm sorry, Katarina." I mumble looking down at my sneakers. I had taken a moment to change before we left. There was no way I was walking the streets of either city in tights and a unitard.

"We've got you." Gregor lays his palm on my shoulder and I sigh at the contact. Having both of them here is a reassurance and support I desperately need.

A few moments later, a van with a party supply logo on the side pulls up and honks at us. Gregor lifts his bag and mine up and indicates we should follow him. An elderly black woman sits in the driver's seat and waves to him, as Gregor opens the panel door and shoves our bags inside.

"Hey baby," she says to Gregor.

"Hi Mom. Thanks for picking us up."

"Sure thing." She looks at Katarina and I as we climb in the back seat.

"Mom, this is Katarina and Colin. I've texted you about them before. Colin's family are the ones…they were injured. We need to get to the hospital," he finishes.

"Of course." She puts the car in drive as Gregor pulls the

door shut and enters traffic that merges onto the main boulevard. She keeps glancing at me in the rearview mirror.

"I'm sorry about your family," she says. Her eyes are the same color as Gregor's. Although her skin is marginally darker, she has straight black hair unlike his curly hair, and she has wrinkles that are pinched near her eyes from stress, laughter, and age.

"Thank you, Ms. McCallum," I murmur.

"Everyone's free to call me Momma J or Janice," she informs us. "My baby has told me a lot about you two. Practically feels like you're a couple of my own."

Katarina's face beams and I offer a small smile. I didn't know Gregor had told his family about us, but it sends a glimmer of hope through my internal cage of despair.

I glance around the van, noting the boxes of party supplies in the farthest back seat. It looks as if they are decorations for a bachelorette party judging by the pink and black satin and frilly material I see peeking out of one of the boxes, and a bachelorette sash that is tumbling out of one of the other boxes.

Janice turns the corner and my attention is drawn back to reality. It has taken us no time at all to navigate the streets of South Boston, despite it being rush hour. If we had needed to walk, it would have taken us at least an hour to hit all of the cross walks that would keep us from getting a ticket for jaywalking, never mind having to lug our bags behind us. Janice seems to know the ins and outs of the street shortcuts, because I see the hospital looming ahead of us on the corner of Broadway and Main.

As she pulls up to the curb she glances back at Gregor, "text me if you need me to come pick you up," she tells him. To Katarina and I she says, "You are welcome to stay with us if you need to. I understand this is a family matter, but the door is always open at the McCallum house. You take care and come by for dinner sometime. I would love to get a chance to get to know Gregor's friends better."

She gives Gregor a pointed look and then smiles warmly at us again.

"Thanks, Janice," I murmur as I get out of the van.

"Thanks, Momma J!" Katarina beams at her.

"Good luck with your family." She looks directly at me, and I have that flash of feeling I get whenever Gregor is around. It fills me with warmth and security, like somehow everything's going to be ok. I nod and shut the door.

When we turn and enter the hospital, the acrid smell of sterility hits my nostrils and I sneeze. I walk to the information desk and ask where the O'Shea rooms are and with a pitying look, the receptionist tells me the floor and room numbers. It must be worse than I thought.

I step into the elevator and press the button for the fourth floor, trauma, and wait while the light flashes between the levels. When the elevator pings and the doors slide open, I see my Mum at the far end of the hall, speaking with a doctor and a nurse.

She glances over and sees me and then begins to run down the hallway toward me, tears streaming down her face.

"Oh, Colin!" she cries. The tears I had been holding back break past the dam of fortitude I had mentally thrown in place, and my throat hurts.

"Mum!" I pull her into a hug as Gregor and Katarina step to the side. As I glance over her shoulder I see my sisters and Aiden split between two adjoining hospital rooms. They look up and tug at one another's sleeves, pointing to Mum and I and Aiden comes running out of the room, arms held up. I scoop him up as I let go of Mum and ask, "Are they going to be alright? How bad is it? What's going to happen now?"

She mops at her face and gives Aiden a peck on the cheek.

"Your father took the worst of the blast. He's got a broken ankle and several shrapnel wounds. The blast knocked him back so far, he ended up with a concussion. Patrick has a broken collar bone and a few cuts and bruises. Seamus and Liam have some cuts and bruises too, but the doctors want to make sure there's no internal bleeding before releasing them. Colin, oh Colin. How did you find out? I told your sisters not to tell you until Christmas break. Your last text about becoming the lead…"

"Mum, this is way more important than a dance. This is family. Of course, I was going to come home when I found out." I realize I'm a little annoyed with her. She's always tried to protect me. "Is Dad...is he going to be able to go back to work?" I ask her.

The look on her face says it all. "At his age, no. Not likely. He has to have a titanium ankle put in and he will always have a limp from now on. It doesn't look good."

"I'm sorry, Mum."

"I know. We're so blessed though. Everyone is going to pull through. I feel for Rose Murphy. She lost her Jimmy. He was the one who...he didn't make it Colin." She trails off, wiping away a fresh round of tears from her eyes. I feel my heart sink. Jimmy and Rose were an older couple that lived upstairs. Mum and Dad had rented an apartment to them for years. Jimmy was only a few years away from retirement and would often ride into work with Dad and my brothers.

I look around numbly, feeling Aiden squirm in my arms. He's trying to get to Katarina who holds out her arms. I hand him over and he promptly begins to tug at her long dark hair. She coos at him and says hello to Mum and that she's sorry. Mum gives her a quick squeeze and that's when I realize she is staring at Gregor.

"Mum this is Gregor, my umm...my friend from school. Gregor, this is my Mum, Molly O'Shea." He holds out his hand and she grasps it but pulls him into a hug too.

"Thank you for getting our Colin home today," she tells him as she lets go.

"You're welcome, Mrs. O'Shea."

We all turn to the rooms where we are greeted by Kathy, Collene, and Sarah. Liam's girlfriend Katie is there, Aiden's mom, and after hugging and introductions, I go in and see Liam and Seamus. Both my brothers are sitting up in bed, watching a game on t.v. when I walk in and both give me lopsided, toothy grins as they greet me. They are almost identical to one another, except the fact that they are a year apart in age. They have the same chestnut hair and broad noses. Their eyes are green like Dad's and their hair is tousled and falls just to their broad shoulders. After visiting with them and feeling a tension in the pit of my stomach lessen, marginally, I leave their room and enter Dad and Patrick's.

Patrick is sitting up in bed and asks, "what are you doing here?"

"I came to see if you were alright," I answer. He stares at me before glancing over my shoulder at Katarina and Gregor who are just inside the doorway. He turns back to the book he was reading without another word, and I sigh, looking over at Dad. He's lying flat on his back with his eyes closed and a bandage around his head. His foot has been elevated and there are cuts and scrapes all over his face and neck. His eye is beginning to form a nasty bruise under the socket and his breathing is ragged and sporadic. I turn to Mum and just as I am about to say something, a man walks in the door. I recognize him immediately from his photographs on the news. James O'Duffy's broad shoulders fill the doorway as my eyes travel up his burly form to his freckled face and ginger hair.

CHAPTER THIRTEEN

"*I* hope I'm not interrupting anything, Molly," James says quietly. His voice is low and rumbles.

"Not at all, Mr. O'Duffy," Mum responds.

I look at her in shock that he seems to be familiar with my Mum. He gives her a pleasant enough smile, but it fills me with dread because it doesn't reach his piercing blue eyes. I notice there are two unfamiliar men standing outside the doorway and my sisters have retreated, probably into Seamus and Liam's room.

"I just spoke with the administration, everything is settled here," he continues. He hasn't looked at Mum but is looking between myself, Katarina and Gregor.

"That is very kind of you, Mr. O'Duffy," she responds.

He moves into the room, looking around, like he is assessing the situation.

"I was hoping to speak with Finn," he comments but no one says anything. "He will be given a generous disability package, of course." He looks out the window into the city streets below.

"Thank you, Sir," Mum whispers. "That is very kind of you."

He turns back to us, smiling. "I have already spoken with Liam and Seamus. And they have indicated they will be back at work in a few days. Patrick, you are of course welcome back once you have healed and we will pay you medical leave for this ah…unfortunate accident."

He says accident but there isn't a person here who doesn't know that the explosion was because of something going on between him and his rivals. He's probably already planning, if not already executing, some sort of retribution for the attack, but none of us are stupid enough to contradict him or question him.

His stare turns back to me and my friends. I introduce them quickly and he chuckles.

"An Irishman, a Russian and a…well, a very unusual group of friends indeed," he murmurs as he shakes hands with all of us. "And will you be joining the O'Shea clan in coming to work at the docks?" he asks.

Patrick begins to speak, "no, Sir. He is…" But before he can finish whatever condemning statement he is about to make, there is a rustling and as my Dad sits up and cuts him off.

"He is my son." He clears his throat. O'Duffy turns around and smiles at him.

"Yes, we were just having introductions. Is he not a tradesman as well?" he asks.

"No. He and his friends go to the school in the city. If it's bodies you need working down at the docks, I'm sure I can find some way to be useful once they put in the new ankle, James." My Dad's voice is firm, and he gives Patrick a pointed look.

There's no denying that a man like James O'Duffy has staunch religious views. He might not be as understanding or turn the other cheek as some do to my lifestyle. That, and the way he spoke about Katarina being Russian and Gregor, hinted that he views people based on such characterizations as ethnicity; it wouldn't be too far fetched for him to take the leap to judge about someone's sexual proclivities.

He looks between Gregor and I and then smiles, "don't you worry about your job, Finn. You've been a hard worker over the years. If we need to find you something, I'm sure we can. Or we can work out an early retirement and disability. You take care now."

He walks past me, giving Mum a kiss on the cheek, and his muscle follows behind him dutifully. The whole room breathes a collective sigh of relief, and then I look at Dad, not sure which I am more grateful for, him being alright, or him defending me to one of the biggest mobsters in the city. My lip trembles but I bite back the tears as I look at him. His face is pale and looks more tired and gaunt than usual, but he gives me a small smile for once when he asks, "Who's your new friend?" He looks at Gregor because he already knows Katarina. Before I can say anything, Gregor steps forward and introduces himself.

"Gregor, Sir. It's nice to meet you."

There's another hare's breath when the entire room wonders if Dad will shake the outstretched hand held out to him, but the last of what feels like the cement block in my stomach loosens as he reaches up with his good arm and clasps his palm.

After we visit for a while we decide the best thing for Dad is some more sleep. Liam and Seamus are coming home tomorrow, and Patrick most likely the day after that. Mum insists we all cram in with the girls into her station wagon, and we set off for the house.

When we get there, Gregor and Katarina stand around in the kitchen, as everyone sets off for various rooms and parts of the house they have laid claim to. Katie pries Aiden off of Gregor, who he had been clinging to for the last hour, bouncing on his knee in the waiting room at the hospital.

"Why don't you show your friends to your room, so they can have a rest?" Mum suggests. "Then you can come back and help me get dinner going." It's Mum's speak for, I need to talk to you but don't want to be rude and ask your friends to wander around a stranger's house.

"Sure, Mum." I've been avoiding making eye contact with her after James O'Duffy left. I hadn't meant to cause more problems by showing up, but I'm worried that I might have.

"Grab the blow-up mattress from the closet for yourself and Katarina can have the futon in your room and Gregor can have the bed," she instructs.

"Thank you, Mrs. O'Shea but that won't be necessary. My Mom's house is only a few blocks from here. Whenever I need to, she said she'd come and get me." Gregor says softly.

"Are you sure? Oh well, please tell your mom I thank her for getting you all here from the train station. We'll have to have her around for dinner sometime. And I insist you stay for dinner tonight. Train sandwiches are no kind of food at all."

No one argues about this, so I walk with Gregor and Katarina through the hallway that leads to the large living room. The space is wide, sporting two couches and an arm chair that is delegated for Dad every night. We pass through the area and Gregor has to duck under the chandelier, even though the ceilings are high. As we pass through the long living room, I cringe at the crown molding that borders the walls near the ceiling. Obviously, my brothers have neglected to help Mum paint, or dust. The corners are filled with cobwebs and peeling paint, despite the long oak table being scrubbed and polished to a shine.

We climb the stairs, which were once the back entrance to the apartment building, and now lead to the farthest two apartments on the second floor, which have been converted into bedrooms. Mine is at the far-right corner of the landing and I let Katarina and Gregor inside. I quickly begin moving boxes that Dad had stored stuff in, out into the hallway, so that they can fit into the room and sit down.

Once in the room, we all sit for a minute, staring at each other, silently.

"So, umm, thank you both for coming with me. And you can see he's going to be ok, so that's good. That's really good," I babble. I fall silent and look around my room which hasn't changed since I left for school. Posters of different destinations around the world are pinned to the yellow walls. I had never dared to hang the posters of my favorite ballet companies, so instead opted for all of the cities I someday wish to travel with a professional company. Gregor is looking around the room with mild curiosity and Katarina flops back onto the futon with an old magazine about Gardening in the City that Mum had shoved into one of the boxes that I had moved. She'd grabbed it on her way into the room and she glances over.

"Like we wouldn't be there for you if you ever needed us," her tone is flippant, but her face is serene. She means every word. I bite my lip as I turn to Gregor, wondering what he is going to say. Before I can say anything, he leans over and gives me a quick kiss on the cheek.

"I think your Mum needed your help," he murmurs softly. I glance back at Katarina who is smiling behind the magazine and get up and walk back downstairs, my insides squirming.

When I enter the kitchen, Kathy is sitting on a stool at the island counter, patting her on the back.

"It's alright, Mum. He's going to be alright. The doctors said so today, it looks like he's out of the woods."

Mum is sobbing into one of her ridiculous aprons that has a pig wearing a chef hat dancing around a meadow on it. I never understood why a pig chef would be in a meadow and not dancing in a kitchen, but I'm not one to judge where anyone dances anymore.

"Mum," I say softly, and she looks up. If there's one thing I cannot stand, it's to see my Mum in tears. It was always hard seeing my sisters cry, especially when one of my older brothers got them going, but when it's Mum, I practically melt. "Mum, don't cry. You heard Kathy. He's going to be alright. He's going to come home."

I walk around the island and place my arms around her as she sobs harder.

"I know. I know he will be. It's just been so much. To get that phone call. Oh Colin, it was awful. All four of them. And I have to bake something for Rose. Someone should go up and check on Rose," she sobs.

Of course, Mum would be thinking of someone else at a time like this.

"Absolutely Mum, someone will go check on her. I suspect her kids have come home and are with her. But someone will go," I reassure her.

Kathy gets up, giving my hand a squeeze and goes to the counter where there is always several jars of freshly baked cookies.

"I'll grab Katarina and we'll go see her together," Kathy suggests. Mum looks up to approve of whichever cookies she has.

"Oh no dear, not the raisin, she doesn't like them. Take the chocolate chip, Jimmy loved them so." A new wave of sobs wracks her body and I hold on tighter as Kathy grabs the cookies and makes her escape.

"I'll send Collene down to help with dinner," she calls over her shoulder.

I sit with Mum a few more minutes while she cries. Sometimes it's best to just let it out. After a few more minutes when her hiccups start, I go to the cabinet above the fridge and grab a glass and the open bottle of Bushmill's and pour her a glass. She doesn't drink much, but now would be just the occasion to help calm her nerves a bit.

She pats me on the hand as she takes the glass and has a sip. She coughs and then sets the glass down.

"I didn't mean to cause more problems, you know, with O'Duffy," I tell her.

"Oh, you didn't. I've been telling your father for years I don't like the idea of him working for a man like that, but there is only a choice between him or that other one. He always told me he keeps his head down and stays out of their business, but a man has got to work."

"Yeah, it's the way this town goes Mum."

"He wanted to be a grocer," Mum blurts out. I raise my eyebrows at this, as it is new to me.

"Really?"

"Yes. Not one of those large supermarkets, but a small corner store where everyone knows everyone else's name. The trouble is, he never took the leap of faith to do it. And now look where it has him." She mops at her face with her apron as she says this.

"Well, it's awful he got hurt, but maybe the one good thing to come of it is that when O'Duffy offers him the early retirement package, he might do it now," I offer. She looks thoughtful for a moment, like she is mulling this over in her mind. Then she nods and stands up.

"Maybe you're right. I'll have to tell him he should do that. Then your brothers can go to work for him." I see the gleam in her eye. Like she's figured out the plan and now she either has to nag, hound, beg, badger, cajole and possibly even blackmail, although she would never admit to it, and work my Dad into such a state that he opens the grocery store, just to shut her up.

I smile as I turn to the cabinets and ask, "So what am I helping to make for dinner."

"You aren't. Collene will. You left your friends alone in your room and that's rude. It would have been fine with Katarina

here, but poor Gregor must not know what to think of us."
She begins bustling around the kitchen. "Go tell him I'm
sorry and keep him company."

I turn and walk back down the hall as Collene enters. There's
no use arguing with her now. She's determined to cook
herself into a frenzy until everything is better. No doubt, she
has already decided which casserole to send up to Rose. The
cookies would have been a pre-funeral feel better dish.

When I get back upstairs, Gregor is stretched out on my bed
with his eyes closed. His faded fedora hat that he likes to
wear is resting on his chest, and I shut the door quietly and
tiptoe to the futon. Before I can sit down, I feel his arm snake
around my waist, and I throw my arms out as I stumble and
fall, collapsing half on top of him onto the bed. He tucks me
under his arm and kisses the top of my head as I lie there,
frozen, while my brain catches up to my bodies response to
jump up and run.

"Easy," he mumbles into my hair. "I don't want anything. I
just think you need a break. You've been running hard ever
since the news broadcast, and you just need to let go and let
someone else steer for a while. Get what I'm saying?"

I do get it. He's offering me a pass from the emotional confusion of being attracted to him. Without the dance at the fore-
front of my mind, there's only two solids keeping me going.
My family and my friends. With the family preoccupied and
the other friend upstairs, all too soon I'd sit down like my
Mum, and have nothing to face except the worry and anxiety
that has been eating away at me since this afternoon.

I relax into his arms and let my head rest on his chest. We're
crammed into my double bed, but we manage to both be on
the mattress. Gregor's hand under my body curls up and

rubs my back and I close my eyes, finally able to let go and relax a little.

"Thank you for being here," I mumble into his chest.

"Wouldn't be anywhere else," he states. "So, I get why there are no dance posters, but why the cities?" He asks a few minutes later as he glances around the room.

"They are all the places I want to travel with the dance companies," I admit.

"Makes sense. Do you ever think you dance because you are trying to escape something? Maybe escape yourself or this city?" he asks nonchalantly. I wonder what exactly he is calling me out on.

"Are you asking because you think I struggle with admitting that I'm gay?" I ask him.

"No. I think you've probably already accepted that about yourself, but maybe you don't fully embrace it. Like, you know you're gay, but you have decided pursuing relationships isn't a priority because it would be an inconvenience to you or your family."

I stare at him, shocked. "Are you seriously going to push this conversation now? After everything that has happened today?"

"You misunderstand me, Colin. I'm not judging you, just asking a question. You show it by displaying the cities you want to escape to. I show it by auditioning for characters that completely take over my life and I get to pretend to be someone I'm not."

I fall silent for a moment, letting it sink in exactly what he is trying to say. Never had I once considered he struggled with his self-identity too. I'd always assumed he chose acting because that was what he was passionate about. I guess we had both been using our vocations as a way to hide. As I turn this over in my mind, he continues.

"Looks like we both were looking for the musical to set us free, huh?" he smiles at me.

"I guess so. I had thought, this piece was alternative, they will want someone who is different for it because it's about showing that differences are ok," I admit. He brings his far arm across his belly and cups my chin. As he tilts my head back, he brings his lips to mine and brushes them across my own. Somehow, the kiss is a testament that we finally have an understanding of one another on some level.

It isn't a hard kiss, and it isn't fast, but it conveys a message and I am grateful for it and allow myself to be swallowed up in it, until Mum calls up a half an hour later that dinner is ready. We break it off and smile at each other as Katarina pokes her head in the door.

"Come on guys, whatever Mum made smells delicious." She grins at us as my face flushes red and Gregor gazes down at me under hooded eyes, but we get up and follow her downstairs.

CHAPTER FOURTEEN

The next few days of the holiday are spent visiting Dad in the hospital; he finally comes home the day after Christmas. I had busied myself when I wasn't at the hospital with helping Mum with things like dusting and repainting the dining room, while Katarina looked after and played with Aiden.

I had snuck the boxes of old magazines from my room downstairs to the dumpster, so that when Mum wasn't home on trash day, she wouldn't notice that they were gone. It ensured I could fit in my room the next time I came home.

Gregor had been in and out, helping me with the small projects. He has remained respectful and not displaying affection when my family was around so that it wasn't awkward for anyone, although they clearly had suspicions on their faces. Near the last day we were going to be staying before we head back to school, Gregor asks, "Would you like to come to my house to meet my family? My mom has been bugging me all week to have you over. She and my sisters have to go do a bachelorette party after, but she would love to get to know you."

"Sure." I look at Katarina wondering why she doesn't seem upset.

"My parents decided to come to the city near school. They're staying in a hotel but want to talk to me. I told them I would see them when I get back, but I've been putting it off all week. I'm headed back to school a day early though. They won't leave until I see them."

"Are you sure you don't want us to go with you?" I ask looking between her and Gregor. He doesn't look upset, but he raises an eyebrow as if to say, "you going to bail on me?"

"No, it's ok. They will want to have this conversation in private, go with Gregor and have fun."

"Ok." I pick up my bag and walk with them downstairs. I explain to Mum what our plan is and she fusses over us for a while, cramming bags of cookies into our bags and making sure we are all set for the next semester. I leave a plain white envelope with her tickets to the show on the island counter when she isn't looking, and Gregor, Katarina, and I walk out the door to the busy street and hail a cab.

We part ways when the cab drops us off in front of another apartment building. Katarina waves to us from the window of the cab as she is taken to the train station. I look up at the many windows of the building wondering which one his Mom's apartment is on.

I soon find out that they are on the top floor, and the elevator is broken.

As we trudge up the stairs, I elbow him and joke, "it's a good thing we are headed back to school tomorrow, all these stairs

128

are showing me how only a week away can get me out of shape."

He grins at me and in between floors, he turns and pulls me into him, planting a hard kiss on my lips. It's possessive and leaves me breathless, the flush begins to crawl up my face. He continues up the stairs and I follow after him, panting from either exertion, or breathlessness from his kiss.

When we finally hit the landing to the top floor, he pulls a key from his pocket and lets us into a pale blue hallway.

"Mom, I'm home!" he calls.

"In here!" she yells back.

We walk into a red and gold decorated living room, and sitting around the t.v. is Janice and who I presume are Joey, Tanya, and Shea. Gregor makes the introductions, confirming my assumption, and I learn Shea is the taller of the two girls and Tanya is shorter and plumper. Joey looks a lot like Gregor, but both girls have attributes, nose shape and the angle of their face, that must be from their dad.

"Hey, it's so nice to finally meet you!" Shea jumps up and holds out her hand.

"Thanks, you too." I shake her hand.

Joey stands up and shrugs his shoulders, holding out his fist. I give him an awkward fist bump and then he sits back down as Tanya steps up to give Gregor a hug.

"Don't mind the little twerp. He's always like that," she comments. Joey seems transfixed on the game show on t.v. and Gregor stoops to give his mom a hug.

"Hi, Janice." I give a little wave and she gets up, pulling me into a hug. She smells like cinnamon and flowers.

"Hello, child. Gregor told me your daddy is going to be ok."

"Yeah, he came home a couple of days ago." My voice is muffled in the crook of her arm, but she beckons us all in the kitchen. Their apartment is considerably smaller than ours, but it isn't any less homey. The source of the cinnamon is a rack of cinnamon rolls cooling on the counter. She sets an extra place setting around the table and we all sit and dig into her dinner of spaghetti and meatballs. I feel bloated by the time I am done eating, and everyone bustles around the kitchen cleaning up. All through dinner Gregor and I fielded questions about the dance and school. They'd asked about what was going to happen with my dad and it all felt very strange to me that they were a family that was so open with one another. My family is very close but there are certain things that just aren't talked about. That isn't the case with the McCallum family. I learn this especially when Tanya says, "It's so nice to meet you. We have all been so excited to meet Gregor's new boyfriend, but he never comes home on the weekends anymore because of the musical."

The rest of the family glances between us as I flush and look at Gregor. I feel more embarrassed that I had introduced him to my family as a friend, and with knowing so little about me, they knew me as his boyfriend.

"Tanya," Gregor chides. "I told you not to be so blunt about stuff."

"You know how we are, Gregor. We just want to see you happy," Janice pipes up.

"I know, Mom." He reaches above her and puts a stack of plates away. "It's just that I told Colin we would go at a pace that he wants, and he doesn't talk openly about this stuff yet," he murmurs.

The family glances at me and gives me a sympathetic smile, but Janice seems to have not heard her son. She looks at me when she says, "Now listen here. There's some things a mother knows. And I always knew my baby was different and I taught him there's nothing wrong with that. My kids have faced a lot growing up for having a white father, especially Gregor. Don't you ever let anyone make you feel bad for being who you are, understand?"

Her face is deadly serious, and I croak, "Yes, Ma'am."

"Alright then. Girls, load up in the van. Joey, if you want to be dropped off at Charlie's house for the night, get your butt in the van too. And I better not catch you roaming in the park again, clear?"

He shrugs, picks up his backpack and gives Gregor a hug. The fist bump this time is less awkward and then he is out the door with Janice chasing after him, the whole while nagging at him about sneaking out of the house. Tanya and Shea give us each a hug and Gregor walks them to the door, shutting it behind him. As he turns back he's grinning as I stand in the middle of the kitchen holding onto the back of a chair.

"So, alone at last," he murmurs.

"Yeah, looks that way," I respond. We stand there in the kitchen, watching each other for a moment before I turn back to the sink. "We should finish helping your Mom with these dishes. You helped me paint the dining room."

I reach into the sink and begin scrubbing plates clean, rinsing them and placing them on the drying rack. I sense Gregor come up behind me, and I feel him brush against my side as he reaches around me and flips a switch on the radio that sits on the shelf.

A low beat strums out of the radio and fills the kitchen. Gregor grabs a dish towel and casually takes a plate from the rack, drying it and putting it away. I scrub harder and faster as I feel my pulse quicken and my breathing becomes more rapid. I had meant to work through the dishes slowly and methodically, but all too soon, there are no more to wash and I'm left leaning over the kitchen sink, watching it drain.

Gregor puts the last glass away in the cabinet and I feel him approach from behind. His arms circle my waist and I shiver as I feel his lips on the back of my neck.

"You can't avoid me forever," he whispers, and I drop my chin to my chest. His lips brush across my skin and I brace my arms on either side of the sink on the counter as I feel him press up against me.

"I'm not avoiding you. I'm just…"

"Scared?" he whispers.

"Umm, yeah maybe a little," I admit.

"I'm not going to hurt you. I keep telling you that, Colin," he murmurs.

I turn in his arms, so I can look at his face. His eyes have that spark in them that I have come to crave. It's when I know he feels truly passionate about something, or someone. Remembering the last time I saw it, I push at his chest.

"Before I…before we do anything, I need to know."

"Seth doesn't mean what you think he does," he answers, anticipating my question.

"Ok, I guess I don't understand then. You are so nice to him, and after what he did to you."

"I'm nice to everyone. It's how Mom raised us. It isn't easy being gay and Milano and in a city that is so segregated sometimes. It's just how I am. It doesn't mean I forgot what he did," he responds.

"Ok, I think I get that. I just don't understand what you want from me."

"I thought I've been pretty clear, Colin. I want you. Just you. Whatever that means you're doing in your life, from painting dining rooms to dancing. If it's what you want to do and its part of who you are, that's what I want." He pulls me back into his arms and I tilt my head back, looking up at him.

"I can't promise I won't push you away some more. I was never looking for a relationship, Gregor," I confess.

"I know. And I'm not going to push you to doing anything you don't want to do. I meant it when I said that. I just want to be here with you, right now." He lowers his head and for once I don't try to pull away. The kiss is soft at first, explorative, but then it quickly transpires into a hot, demanding kiss that is urging me for more. Gregor's kiss may be conveying what he wants, but his hands remain firmly where they had circled around my waist, and he stays true to his word, not demanding more. It's me that begins to let my hands roam, realizing it has been so long since we had explored one another on the rooftop, and I want nothing more, now, than to feel his skin on mine.

I claw at his t-shirt and he steps back, whipping it up and over his head. He bunches it and tosses it into the corner as he half drags me towards the living room, still lip-locked. We stumble over chairs and bump into shelves as the urgency to be with one another grows and grows into something that is frantic and needy.

I nip at his bottom lip and the sound that comes from him is half moan, half growl as we stumble, tripping on the stairs up to his bedroom. He grabs at my t-shirt and I in turn whip it up over my head, just as he had done. His hands are running all over my torso and my mind has turned to complete neediness for this man. The things he does to me, the way he makes me feel. Like I'm the only man in the world who could ever make him happy. It's intense and scary at the same time and I don't understand it. It's just that if I don't have him in some way, and very soon, it will feel like I am falling apart.

The feelings have gone beyond just physical attraction. I started off not wanting to get involved with Gregor. He was a passing fancy, but the more I got to know him, and the more I let his infectious enthusiasm enter my life, the more I began to fall for him.

Gregor pushes his bedroom door open and I hardly notice the green and silver wallpaper. I think it's flowers of some kind, but I don't comment. I don't care. All I care about is having him and having him now.

I reach for the zipper of his jeans as we collapse onto the bed, and when I shove the jeans down on his hips, I reach between us and begin stroking him. His chest is rising and falling as I try to convey through my massage just how much I need and want him. His eyes roll back when my palm brushes over the head of him, gathering the moisture that was there and letting it help my palm glide down over him. I let my hand rub in small, short jerks as I lean up and initiate the next kiss. He tries to take control, but I always succumb to his kisses. This time he needs to know how much I want and appreciate him.

I pull my head back when he tries to dominate the kiss, he stares up at me, confused. I lower my head back down and begin exploring his lips with my own. I dart my tongue in between them and massage his tongue, letting him now that I want him and that I want to know him.

I break off the kiss and explore the length of his neck, kissing, nipping and tasting while I continue to stroke him with my palm. He reaches for me several times, but I pull back so his hands grip the green comforter of the bed instead. As my mouth works back down his chest and stomach, he grabs the back of my head and I hold still.

"Can't," he gasps. "Can't hold on much longer this time."

I'd teased him mercilessly on the rooftop. This time was proving to be even more intense. We'd been skirting around one another for weeks, this was about discovering and possessing, not wooing and teasing.

"Do you have anything?" I ask the question and he pulls open the nightstand drawer. The red display on the clock reads eight o'clock. It's still early for us to be interrupted. I fish around in the assortment of items at the bottom of the drawer and find what I need. I stand and quickly shove my jeans down my waist, putting on what I had grabbed.

When I am ready, I kneel behind Gregor who has turned on his side. He's breathing hard as he watches me over his shoulder, and I kiss him, reassuring him that this is what I want.

I press into him and he moans, arching his hips back to me so that it makes it easier. Never in a million years did I think I would be the one to instigate this, but it makes me feel powerful as I take charge. I grab his hips and ease myself inside him. He's so tight and I've never felt a pressure quite like it. I go slow, not wanting to hurt him. Never having done this, I'm not sure of the right pace, until he begins to move back and forth, rocking himself on me and pushing me in deeper.

It takes me a few moments to match the rhythm and motion, but when I finally find a pace that works for both of us, I reach around with my free hand and continue stroking him. He gasps when my fingers close around him, and I feel his erection kick in my hand as his pulse pumps faster and faster. He turns his head into his pillow and I nip the back of his neck, just as he had done to me in the kitchen. I then leave a hot trail of kisses to his earlobe where I suck on his skin, just under his ear.

I can't keep the pace up much longer as I rock into him, back and forth. The friction is causing the ache from way down low to start spreading through me. I can feel the tingling through my nerves, and the pinching starts in the back of my neck as the throbbing starts to take over.

How can being with one man cause me to lose all control? My brain is firing rapidly, telling me to go faster and faster, but I hold back, not wanting to hurt him. I drop my head to his shoulder and kiss his skin, as small beads of sweat break out all over his skin. I can feel the same on mine as we rock into one another and I'm getting to that place where the franticness is taking over and I need to do something, anything, for the final leap in order to drop over the edge of this bliss.

Sensing what I so desperately need, Gregor clenches around me and my eyes pop open as I finally topple over in an explosion of pure bliss. I thrust my hips one last time, clinging to him and around him as I feel him spill over into my hand in front of me. His cries mingle with my own as we shudder and pant in the aftermath.

After a few moments he rolls over in my arms and draws me to him. He bends his head and I lean up, kissing him softly.

"You chose me," he murmurs. I think about this for a moment. I had never once anticipated that I would be the one to instigate this.

"Yeah, I did," I whisper.

"Do you um, do you regret it?" he asks.

"Not at all," I admit. He hugs me tighter and we lie in each other's arms for a few more moments before getting up and cleaning up.

Gregor makes his way downstairs to grab his t-shirt and I wash my hands in the bathroom. I don't hear him come up behind me, until I feel his lips press to my ear.

"We need to loosen up before practice tomorrow," he murmurs.

"How do you propose we do that?" I ask, chuckling because the rasp of his beard tickles.

"Get dressed, you know I've always needed a rooftop view."

With that, I follow him out of the bathroom and hastily dress. He leads me up to the rooftop of his apartment building, which isn't as far of a climb as the one back at Julliard since we are already on the top floor. From here we sway in each other's arms as we take in the sites of the Boston skyline at night. Much like New York, the lights twinkle in a way that reminds me of fairy lights, and also resemble the light that dances in Gregor's eyes whenever he is in a good mood.

We don't stay on the rooftop long. Boston in December is chilly, and we make our way back down to the apartment.

He has a message on his phone from his Mom saying she won't be home tonight because she'd had too many glasses of champagne with the girls and we smile at one another realizing we have the whole apartment to ourselves for the night.

At around midnight and after I had given myself over to Gregor, having taken the place of him from before, we make our way back to the bathroom and fill the large claw foot tub with hot water. I'm not usually one to take a bath, preferring quick efficient showers, but I realize as I doze off to sleep in Gregor's arms in the warm water, there isn't anywhere I would rather be than right here and right now.

CHAPTER FIFTEEN

The next day we head back to school on the train and I have no hesitation about holding Gregor's hand in public. We even steal kisses once we are seated on the train and laugh when he tells me jokes about his sisters and brother growing up. I realize for the first time I am the friend I had envied when I spied on him in the dining hall. I am the person he is laughing and joking with and it feels like being wrapped in warmth.

When we get back to school, it is hard to part ways with him, but I want to check in with Katarina and hit the barre to begin working my way back into dancing. I'd done small exercises throughout the week to keep my tone and form, but it was going to be a strenuous couple of weeks catching up and getting back to full form.

I plunk my bag down on my bed and grab my shoes before heading downstairs. I look around the barren walls and fish my cell phone out of my pocket.

"Hey, can you come up here?" I text Katarina.

"Sure, be there in a minute," is her reply. I unzip my bag and begin unrolling long, pristine posters of my favorite ballet companies, and standing on my bed, I start to tack them up on the walls one by one.

"Hey, you, how's it going?" I chirp down at her between clenched teeth. I'm holding one of the tacks in my mouth and I don't want to swallow it.

"Ok, what are you up to?" She climbs up on the bed and smooths her hand over the poster, holding it in place while I tack it up.

"Decorating," I tell her.

"Well, it's about time," she teases.

"So how did the meeting go with your parents?" I glance sideways at her. She bites her lip and pushes the tack in on her side, remaining quiet for a moment.

"Well, I convinced them to come to the Valentine's Day Virtuoso and see me perform. I know I only have a small role, but I want them to see me acting before they completely make up their minds to shut me out."

"That's great!" I exclaim. "It's definitely a start!"

"Yeah maybe," she says. "I'm not entirely convinced they are on board, but at least they will come."

"Well, I think it's fantastic," I tell her.

"How's your dad?" she follows up.

"He's hanging in there. It's going to be a long time before he can walk again after they put in the new ankle. They want to make sure his concussion is fully healed before they put him under. He keeps trying to hobble around the house on one foot with a busted arm and he's driving Mum insane because he won't let her dote on him."

"So, business as usual then?" she asks, and I laugh. She pauses and stares at me. "There's something different, Colin. Something you aren't telling me. I haven't heard you laugh this much since last year at the beginning of school."

I smile and grab another poster and we move a step down the bed. "Oh my God!" she cries. "You and Gregor?" She begins jumping up and down on my bed and squealing with excitement.

"Yeah. Last night at his place," I mumble as my cheeks redden.

"Tell me everything!" Her enthusiasm is infectious, and I grab her arms as we jump up and down. "Ok, not everything, but oh my gosh, yay!" she shouts. Her ponytail bounces behind her and we flop back down onto the bed.

"It was perfect," I confess.

"Well duh, silly," she laughs, and I hit her with a pillow.

"I wasn't looking for anything Katarina. You know that."

"Yeah but what's all that hype about finding someone when you aren't looking in the first place. Finding happiness in yourself first and all that."

"Yeah, I guess so."

"Well it works for gay men too," she retorts.

"I know. It's all so new and then there's the performance to think about and how I'm going to finally tell my family I am seeing someone. It's just a lot."

"None of that matters, don't you get it? You're happy for once." She nudges me with her shoulder.

"Yeah, I guess you're right," I reply. We catch our breath and then she helps me hang the rest of the posters.

When we're done, I give her a hug and head to the studio. It's empty, so I put on some music and begin warm up exercises at the barre, stretching and loosening up, because Gregor had been right. I'm sore in places I didn't realize I would be.

I begin working through a few relevé exercises, when I hear the door to the studio open and shut. I turn around and see Eric standing near the door on his crutches.

"So, you think everything has fallen into place now huh? You've got the lead, you've got the guy, life must just be perfect for you?"

The angry glint in his dark hazel eyes has me worried. Whatever he is plotting is going to be deeply unpleasant for me, I can just see it in the shaking of his shoulders because he is so mad.

"Eric," I greet him, walking over to my water bottle. "Have a good Christmas?" I ask.

I don't see any way out of this confrontation, but that doesn't mean I don't need a minute to collect my thoughts. This is going to be extremely unpleasant.

"You think you've won?" There's a note of hysteria in his voice that has me glance up and look at him from the mirror.

"I wasn't trying to win anything, Eric. You got the lead, fair and square. Then you got injured. That happens sometimes. We're dancers, we know this can happen at any point to any one of us."

I whirl around and face him as he walks over to me.

"If I get out of this cast in time, I will see to it that you don't get to stay on as lead. I am going to make your life hell, do you hear me? For the next few weeks, I am going to be all over your ass in rehearsals and practice. You will wish you had never dared to take the lead role from me."

"I didn't take anything from you Eric and you know it. You were so stuck up, thinking you were better than everyone that it made you cocky. You didn't stretch properly and take into account that not all the dancing is ballet and you got yourself injured. The only thing I took was the ability to step up and try. I am trying to be the best dancer for this lead and if you can't handle that, it's not my problem, so back off!" I shout at him.

I don't anticipate it, but I definitely feel when his fist cracks into my jaw. My teeth clack together so hard, I bite my inner cheek and gasp, swallowing blood.

"You and Gregor! How long do you think that will last? Not even Seth could withstand my seduction. It won't be long before I have Gregor and then we'll see who's taken whom!" he shouts back.

"You stay away from him!" I snarl. "He's my boyfriend!"

Eric looks like I smacked him just now. The shock on his face is plain as day before it contorts into something almost manic.

"Game on," he comments before turning around and walking out the door. I'm so angry I have to pace a few laps around the studio before I can regulate my breathing again. My jaw aches and when next I glance in the mirror, I can see the shiner already starting to form. Great, when Madame sees this she's liable to give me one on the other cheek so that they match and then tell me to cover them with rouge, so they look intentional. I snort at myself. Hardly, Madame is a lot of bluster, but I have come to realize she has a heart of gold.

I continue through my exercises once I have calmed down and work on stretching myself out. When I am done, I work slowly through the choreography of the dances and correct my form. I don't want to push myself too hard, and cause myself injury, so after a couple of hours of practice, I call it a night and return to my dorm where I find Gregor waiting with dinner.

Gregor takes one look at my jaw and then storms toward the door.

"Who did it? Eric?" he demands.

"It doesn't matter," I insist as I pull open a bag of food. It has been so long since I had Chinese food, the savory smell wafts up to my nostrils as I open a carton of noodles. I fish around in the bag but only come up with chopsticks. "Are there any forks?" I ask, looking up at him.

Gregor is standing over me, seething. "What do you mean it doesn't matter? Of course, it matters. He hit you!"

"Well, yeah, but that's only because I told him you are my boyfriend and if he has a problem with that, he can take a hike."

Gregor blinks down at me. "You told him I am your boyfriend?"

"Yep. Is there an issue with that?" I ask.

"Not at all. I am just surprised. Apart from Katarina, you haven't told anyone."

"Yeah, about that. I'm really sorry, Gregor. It hasn't been you, it's just, my family isn't as open as yours. They have some pretty set views, if you know what I mean."

He sits down next to me on the bed and grabs a carton of rice. "I get it, it's ok. In time," he says as he pops the top of his carton.

I struggle with the chopsticks, never having used them. That is until Gregor takes pity on me and wraps the noodles on the stick for me and holds them out. It feels strange to me, to be fed by someone else, but he grins at me and teases, "for one of the most graceful ballet dancers I have ever met, you eat like a pig."

I slurp the noodle that was hanging out of my mouth and stuck to my chin. "As one of the most graceful ballet dancers you have ever met, I make it a habit to eat healthy. I don't typically go for Chinese food. It's fattening and doesn't give a lot of energy to the body for dancing."

"Yeah, Katarina told me about the dancing hippos. Fantasia? Really? Besides, she said she is working on putting some padding on your skinny ass. It's bony."

"You weren't complaining about it last night," I retort. He gets a heated glint in his eye and sets the carton on my night-stand. It's going to leave grease prints, but I'll deal with them later. He takes my carton and sets it next to his, and then tackles me on the bed.

"I'm not complaining," he murmurs as he lowers his head, so his lips meet mine. "I just enjoy getting you riled up. When you feel something intensely, you get all flustered and then that blush reddens your face up and it's sexy." He kisses me as I realize the blush is creeping into my cheeks. First his teasing does exactly that, riles me up. Then my body reacts in a different way and riles itself up. Before I know it, we are in bed again together, the food cartons lying forgotten and all thoughts of Eric gone from our minds. That is, until the next few weeks prove to be just as hellish as Eric promised.

CHAPTER SIXTEEN

$\mathcal{T}$he week of the performance arrives, and Gregor and I have barely found enough time to see each other except to collapse into bed together at night. Katarina acts as a buffer between us, when the performance threatens to ruin our new relationship, and especially when Eric implants himself between us on as many occasions as he can think of.

I have to take a walk when he breaks us apart for our kissing scene and tells me there is no passion and that I need to do it like this…

I see red when he cups Gregor's cheeks and begins kissing him. It's sad to say that I had been looking forward to this particular rehearsal all week, because it would give us the chance to hold one another again in a way that isn't sleeping.

When he breaks off the kiss and steps back, smirking, I seriously consider giving him the shiner he gave me which is now faded to a puce color. I'm not worried about covering it at this point, as all performers will be sent to makeup and that entails a heavily caked on layer of makeup that can distinguish our features from the harsh white stage lighting. It will be well covered. I refuse to look at Eric when he taunts, "You need to do it like that. A lead must show he is the lead by his actions."

I capture Gregor's gaze and he looks as pissed off as I feel.

"Perhaps I should show you again," Eric steps toward Gregor, who holds up his hand.

"We've got it. We don't need your help with this." Eric steps back and Gregor pulls me toward him. I can't help the pout that threatens my lip. I have never felt so jealous even though Gregor clearly didn't appreciate Eric's little stunt.

Gregor pulls me into a kiss that has the whole room fanning themselves and Mr. Schlewp clearing his throat after a few moments. Eric slinks away like the vermin that he is as I stare wide-eyed and flushed at Gregor. I only snap out of my reverie when I hear Madame proclaim, "Mon Dieu, c'était magnificent!"

I glance around and Katarina giggles as I stagger toward my water bottle when Gregor lets me go.

"Yes, I think the two of you need little coaching in er…" Mr. Schlewp busies himself with his script and indicates everyone should take it from the top.

Angela glares at us as she walks over to whisper to Eric, but jumps when Madame barks, "Angela, back in your place!"

Feeling vindicated I take my place and we run through the script, again and again and again until I am singing the songs in my head at night and my feet move under the sheets to the choreography. Gregor threatens to strap me down to the bed and I roll over facing the wall and mutter, "Promise?"

We don't sleep much that night.

The next day is the day before the performance, and after another run through of Swan Lake with Angela hissing in my ear the entire time, we then move on to have one more run through of Rent, and then we are given the evening off.

I quickly excuse myself from the dining hall, telling Gregor I want to go to a fitting one last time because it felt like the seems on my unitard were a little snug and if it needs to be let out then it should be done tonight. He frowns at me and says, "Are you sure? You've tried on that white monstrosity for Swan Lake hundreds of times."

"Yeah, I need to be sure," I tell him, giving him a kiss on the cheek. Everyone around the table is subdued. Not melancholy but just exhausted. The music kids who usually play a little during meals don't even play around with their instruments, and whoever didn't get a part in the musical has been working nonstop backstage on props and set designs and curtain call schedules. The whole dining hall has a hushed feeling to it, like it's waiting for the other shoe to drop. Julliard had even contracted with the Culinary Institute of America to come in and cater the dining tables as part of their midterm practical tests. The menus had been designed and set by them, and the two institutions were working in tandem to put on one of the finest performances between the two schools that the city had ever seen. Crews were working round the clock to transform the auditorium so that small dinette sets were seated between every two seats, but enough room was allowed for the wait staff to use the row below it to maneuver and not obstruct the view of the dances and the musicals. Some of the finest dinery was brought in and the auditorium was grossly over decorated in pinks and reds for the holiday.

The whole atmosphere was one of exhaustion paired with excitement and topped with anticipation as we waited for tomorrow evening. I made my way through the cafeteria to murmured, "good lucks" and "break a leg tomorrow." The only ones who didn't say anything to me were Angela and Eric.

Eric had been in a perpetual bad mood since the rehearsal with the kissing. He had gone to Madame after practice that day and asked to be reinstated as lead, but she had shut him down immediately, telling him he was far too behind to even be considered for it. She reassured him he would be allowed to dance for the end of year performance, which no one else was thinking about at the current time, but he had stormed out of the studio in a fit of rage.

He had been glowering at us all week and offering very little words of advice about the dances, as he was supposed to be doing. Katarina said, "I think he assumes if he doesn't offer any input, you'll make an ass of yourself."

"It's just as well. Madame and Mr. Schlewp have been on my case since I got back," I respond.

Even Gregor seemed unusually quiet and that is why I was leaving in a hurry tonight. He had been worried all week about a particularly difficult move in the choreography and we had been going over it again and again until we were both sick of it.

"Katarina, can you help me?" I ask, looking at her pointedly.

"Can't you do it yourself? It buttons up the front anyway," she whines, pushing her mashed potatoes around on her dinner plate.

"I could really use your help this time," I beg her in earnest.

She glances up and my eyes flutter to Gregor quickly and then back to her.

"Yeah, ok. I wasn't really wanting this anyway," she mutters. She gets up and dumps her tray, returning it to the dish cart and follows me out the door.

When we get to the atrium, I turn right and head toward the front doors.

"Hey, where are you going?" she asks as she hurries to catch up. "I thought you wanted to try on the Swan Lake unitard?"

"I personally would love to burn that material in a fiery blaze if I could, but it will have to be after tomorrow night," I inform her.

"Then where are we going? Colin, I'm exhausted."

I glance over my shoulder to make sure Gregor hasn't followed us or seen us. She keeps pestering me until we are around the corner and halfway down the street.

"I need something for tomorrow," I tell her.

"What could you possibly need for tomorrow? The school is taking care of the costumes and food and stuff," she gripes.

"No, you don't understand. I have never given a Valentine before," I inform her.

"Huh?" She looks confused and I wait for her brain to catch up.

"You want to get something for Gregor!" Her face lights up.

"Yeah, except, I have never gotten a man a Valentine's Day gift, and I have no idea what to get him." I rub the back of my neck. The February chill seeps through my clothes and I want to get back to school and find Gregor to warm up.

"Oh, there are so many options!" She claps her hands together, pulling her light cardigan over her shoulders. I hadn't grabbed outdoor wear, not wanting to give Gregor a suspicion that I was going out. But that was a stupid idea, given how cold it is.

"Let's get inside this little trinket store." She points to a small store on the corner. We enter the shop and a small bell chimes overhead. We rub our hands together and shiver, pressed together for warmth.

"I thought about going to the drug store or supermarket one street further. I'm sure they have cards and chocolate and stuff," I whisper. The store is dimly lit with soft glowing candles. It reminds me of a flower shop, only this one houses all sorts of baubles and knick knacks. There's necklaces and candles for sale. There's incense sticks which make my nose burn and small figurines. It's kind of a catch all store where someone might find something for anyone. I'm hoping maybe I can find something here for Gregor. There's a small display of Valentine items on a table near the register, and it doesn't take me long to pick out a card.

"You think this is good?" I ask Katarina.

"Yeah, that's a good start. But you want something unusual. The relationship you two have isn't ordinary and Gregor is an extraordinary guy!" She's looking around and picks up a pewter elephant.

"I don't know that Gregor has mentioned anything about liking elephants, Katarina." I set the figure down and at that moment, a thin, frail woman with too much perfume and makeup on emerges from the back room through a clinking of beads that cloak the door in long strands. Katarina and I stare up at her as she floats toward us in a rustle of satin. She's wearing a corset dress that belongs circa the Renaissance era and she sashays from side to side as she approaches us. My theory is she's on something, or this is all for dramatic effect, in which case, I truly believe Julliard should offer her a scholarship.

"Hello, dearies," she trills in a sing song voice. "Let me see, you need, a love spell."

"Huh?" Katarina stares at her stupidly. Of all the places in the city we could have stepped into, a faux fortune teller's head shop had to be the one.

"Um, no Ma'am. I'm just looking for a gift for my boyfriend," I tell her. She pauses her swaying and looks at me down her reedy thin nose for a moment.

"Ah!" she cries. "I have just the thing!" She pulls out from under the glass counter, a large display of assorted rings. Most of which are gaudy and pewter.

"Um, I don't think this is quite what I'm looking for," I mutter. I feel my face flush, not wanting to offend her but not really sure I am going to find something that is suitable. "Maybe I should just get the card." I hold it out to her and she places it on the counter.

"Nonsense. There must be something in my wares that you seek."

"Yeah, ok, Shakespeare. We'll just be looking over here." Katarina tugs on my arm as she moves us toward the far display.

"Look, let me just get the card and we can go, ok?" I whisper looking back at the store owner.

"Oh, come on, Colin, pick something out. You dragged me down here in the cold, remember?"

I bite my lip and look around. He wouldn't be into the assorted candles and fragranced oils. I see a display to my right that hosts a bunch of pins. I turn away and look at the scarves and pillows and trinkets lining the shelves. There's nothing here that catches my eye. I turn back to Katarina to beg her to run for it with me, when something flashes in my peripheral vision. It's annoying, so I turn toward the board of pins and see that it is a small silver pin with the theater masks comedy and tragedy set on a silver pin clasp. The back of the masks rests on a bed of two quail feathers that jut up. I suddenly have just the idea and inspiration I have been looking for.

"That," I point to it and turn to the store owner who has danced her way toward us.

"Oh, that old thing? It's dreadful," the store owner comments.

"No, it's perfect," I tell her. "My boyfriend is a theater student at Julliard." She gives me a withering look but moves the entire display, unpinning it from the board. After she rings up the purchase and gift wraps it at the counter, Katarina and I dash up the street back to school, glad to be rid of the assaulting aromas from the store. I was starting to get a headache from the various smells and the store owner kind of creeped me out. When I get back to the school I sit in Katarina's room, trying to think of something to write in the card. I eventually just put the pen to the paper, and let the ink dance across the card.

Dear Gregor,

I've never gotten anyone a Valentine's Day card or gift before. This is a first for me. I wasn't sure what to write, and it seems I'm still not really sure what to say except, thank you. Thank you for being endlessly patient with me. To be honest, I was never looking for a relationship when I first met you. I was so wrapped up in where I thought my life needed to be, I never once considered where it is now and who is in it that makes me happy. But then you came along and changed all of that. You showed me a world where I could dance just for the love of dance again. And you showed me that sometimes the beat and rhythm don't always go to the tempo I want them to, but you taught me that it's ok to change my pace to match it. You taught me that loving someone is a new kind of dance. I realize it hasn't been easy. I've been particularly obtuse. There have been moments we've laughed and cried and probably wanted to scream at each other. That's why I thought this pin would be a great Valentine's gift. Maybe you could pin it to your Fedora? I think it would make a great decoration at the base of the hat and spruce it up a little. The masks, comedy and tragedy, represent us all as we go through life. Our relationship, in particular, has been a comedy of errors. But until you came along, I didn't realize that was the point. That is how relationships are supposed to be. So, I guess what I'm trying to say is that I love you. I love to laugh and cry with you and I can't imagine life without you in it, doing both of those things with me. I think this is the part where I am supposed to ask you to be my Valentine, but truthfully, I feel more like asking you to be my everything.

Love,

Colin

I finish the letter in the card in small cramped writing, and Katarina looks over my shoulder with tears streaming down her face.

"Cut it out," I gripe.

"That's so sweet!" she wipes at her cheeks.

"Yeah, yeah," I shrug and stuff the card in the envelope. I stand and pull her into a hug and then leave the room, cramming the card and the gift box in my bag and head back to my room. When I get there, Gregor is sound asleep, so I carefully unzip my bag, and place the card and the box on top of his hat, knowing he will find them right away when he wakes up. I crawl into bed with him and fall asleep as I warm up under the covers.

CHAPTER SEVENTEEN

The next morning, I wake up and two realizations hit me. The first is that today is the day. The performance is here at last. I feel the weight of anxiety pressing down on my shoulders. I roll out of bed, aware of the second thing which is, Gregor isn't in bed with me anymore. I panic a little until I see a small heart shaped box, sitting on my nightstand. I pick it up and open it.

Inside the box is a set of small silver keys. I frown down at them for a moment before realizing exactly what they are. I pull on my clothes and dash up the countless flights of stairs and try out the first key. It doesn't work so I try the second key which opens the door to the rooftop access.

I prop the door open and run across the roof, hugging my arms to my chest against the cold to where Gregor stands waiting for me. The pin is already on the hat and the card is sticking out of his coat pocket. He doesn't say anything, and I jump into his arms in a hug. After a few moments I lean back for my morning kiss, and when he pulls back he frowns at me.

"Are you nuts? Where is your jacket? You know it's cold up here."

"I forgot when I realized what the key is for," I tell him sheepishly. He pulls me back in his arms and wraps me in his coat to keep me warm while we watch the sun come up over the city. "So, you liked the present?" I ask tentatively.

"It's the best present anyone has ever given me," he admits before leaning in for another kiss.

"Happy Valentine's Day," I mumble into his lips and he smiles. "What's the other key for?" I ask suddenly.

"Oh, I know once you've seen one rooftop, you've seen them all, but the other key is for the rooftop in Boston," he informs me. It's my turn to smile, it seems they are infectious today.

"Rooftops are our place we can go to be on top of the world together," I murmur. He nods in agreement as we look at the city scape. After a few moments and my uncontrollable shivering, he says, "Come on. Time to go get ready."

We make our way downstairs and spend the rest of the day with the other students and Mr. Schlewp and Madame in a state of mind numbing fear and panic. A few times I get so worked up, but then am grateful that Gregor is right there, kissing me and bringing me back down to earth.

That evening, I peek from behind the curtain and the entire auditorium is full. Apparently, a performance and liaison with another school hasn't happened quite like this before. I turn back, unable to find Gregor, because he is in makeup, and instead find a smiling Madame standing in front of me.

"Remember, O'Shea. Just try," she encourages. Her words are every bit as grounding as Gregor's kisses, because for the first time in a long time, I realize that there are people who believe in me.

When it's time to perform Swan Lake, I do it flawlessly. Angela is the picture of perfection and we float and glide across the dance floor. She seems to have given up her hostility, in favor of the romantic vibes from the dining audience. We are applauded to a deafening and uproarious cacophony of sounds. Even Eric can find nothing to critique.

"Did you see? In the audience?" Katarina whispers to me.

"Who?" I ask.

"Only the head of the New York Ballet Company, The American Ballet Company, The Russian Ballet Company and of course, the president here at Julliard. You will have your pick of companies to dance for if you want!" She dances on her toes in excitement as I look at Madame who for the first time, looks at me approvingly.

Our next performance, Rent, leaves not a single person with a dry eye in the house. I dance and sing and deliver my lines to perfection. The rest of the cast and crew perform just as well, and there is a solid minute of complete silence when the curtain falls for the last time, and then the standing ovation has the entire auditorium shaking because the applause, cheers, and whistles are so loud. We move to make our bows and I clasp Gregor's hand as we walk on stage in front of everyone to make our bow. Then in front of the whole auditorium and out of character, he swoops me up and kisses me. The cheering grows louder as flowers and small gifts are thrown up on the stage. We bow again and exit to the right.

When it is all over and family is mingling with performers. Katarina has gone to find her parents and Gregor's mom with her youngest son, Joey, as her date come to congratulate us. But what really surprises me is when I hear a soft voice clear his throat behind me. I whirl around and come face to face with my dad. My jaw drops as I say, "Dad? What are you doing here?" I shake my head as Gregor remains by my side, not saying a word. Dad looks between us and then does something I haven't seen in a long time. He smiles and holds out his arms.

"You were incredible," he says gruffly into my hair when I move in for a hug.

"I didn't know you'd come," I step back. He's leaning heavily on a cane. I had called Mum the week after getting back to school and the surgery had been a success. It was going to be a long time before he could walk without the cane, and he would always have a limp.

"Your mum had the tickets, and to be honest, I really didn't want to miss this," he admits.

"You didn't? I don't understand, you've never said...I didn't think..." I look between him and Gregor who continues to remain silent.

"I spent so many years trying to remain passive about it. But I knew. I wasn't sure how to act, Colin. I was never angry. Then with the explosion, I thought, why am I keeping that from you. You have gone after what makes you happy and by not admitting my approval, I was denying that small bit of it to you. All I've ever wanted was for my sons to be happy. Seeing you dance, and with Gregor here, I realized that you are happy, and that's what's important."

I try so hard to fight the tears in my eyes, but they mist over. "I'm so glad you came," I whisper.

"Me too, son. Me too." He pulls me in to another hug and the last bit of heartache I had been holding in all these years vanishes. I clear my throat, "Where's Mum?"

"She wanted to meet Katarina's parents and Gregor's mom," he admits. I nod and turn to Gregor.

"Um, you remember my dad." He nods and holds out his hand, but my dad pulls him into a hug too.

"Good to see you again, Gregor. You're welcome home with Colin anytime." I see Gregor wipe at his cheeks with his sleeve too.

"I know these are usually saved for female ballerinas and everything, but I wasn't sure what to get male ballerinas."

"Danseurs, we're called Danseurs, Dad." He nods and hands each of us a single red rose. It's touching. "Thank you." I smile at him happily as Gregor loops his arm over my shoulder.

Mum comes up and hugs each of us in turn and we all walk toward the exit as the stage lights dim and go out. Once they are in the taxi to the train station, I turn back to Gregor, my boyfriend, and kiss him in front of the school. We hold each other for a long time, watching the taxi move down the street before turning back to go upstairs. I squeeze his hand, grateful to be so loved and have him at my side while I follow my dreams and dance. Now I know I will always be dancing for his desire, and I am happy with that.

Made in the USA
Monee, IL
12 September 2020

42260186R00095